The LAST ATLANTEAN

EMILY HAYSE

Moxie: force of character, determination, having a fighting spirit.

I spent a summer once working for a lady down the road who talked about facing down her troubles as a young working wife during the Great Depression with her "nineteen-year-old moxie." When I heard that, I knew I needed to write a book about a girl with that nineteen-year-old moxie. This is that book.

PART ONE

Maine, 1912

From the west, the sun will rise

ONE

The Storm off Roke Point

Black storm clouds knotted like an old fisherman's brow as Hattie
Scrow took her shawl down from the hook and opened the brass-bound
front door of the cottage. The wind nearly took the door from her hand
and slammed it open, but she threw her body into holding it back and it
came round like a skiff in the wind.

She locked it with the great brass key that hung on a chain around
her neck, then hurried across the spit of sand and pebbles to the
lighthouse that stood a hundred yards off. The lights towered above her,
pushing against the clouds and spray, bright in the darkening sky.

She ran up the steps and pulled the door open, slamming it behind
her.

"Hattie?" Her father's deep voice rose in response to the slam of
the door.

"Yes, Father!"

"Hattie, bring up the rags and the rest of the can of oil. I'm a little
low."

"Right away!" She went to the old seaman's trunk along the rough
stone wall and propped open the lid, pulling out rags, stuffing them in
the pockets of her skirt, and hefting the large can of kerosene.

"Hattie-girl?"

"Not to fear, Father! I can manage!" She gathered her long skirt in
one hand and mounted the narrow, twisting steps.

He met her at the top of the stairs, reaching out to take the oil and
give her a hand up the last step.

"You must be careful, Hattie-girl." Her father smiled warmly in the flickering light, tweaking her cheek gently in sea-worn fingers.

"Really, Father. You know me. I've been going up and down these stairs all my life. I could do this in the inky black."

"To be sure."

She brushed a windblown strand of hair triumphantly out of her face. "And don't tell me the boys could have done better."

"If I told you that, it wouldn't be the truth." Her father grinned.

He opened the can with a rusty crowbar that had hung on a peg near the lights as long as Hattie could remember. Outside the window, everything was gray-blue and mottled with the brewing storm; the sea was restless, biting at the limey rocks like an uneasy dog gnawing at a bone.

"Is it going to be bad?" She picked up a rag and wiped at a smear on one of the window panes out of habit.

"Bad enough." Her father's eyes were fixed on the oil he was pouring out carefully into the lamp.

"Poor souls," she whispered. "God keep them."

The ocean answered with a crash of wave and spray against the rocks below.

Her father glanced over his shoulder. "We have three ships due in port. The *Good Hope*, the *Wendover,* and another Simon could not remember." He chuckled. "His mind's getting so it has as many holes as his nets."

Hattie had to stand up for the old man. Simon was as much a part of Roke Point as the wharf or the old lighthouse itself. "He still remembers the name of every ship launched from this dock fifty years ago. And his heart's as stout and kind as it ever was."

"You've always been softhearted for him." Her father's eyes gentled. "And I can't say he doesn't deserve it. The best sorts of men are those that keep their good nature when everything else starts to go."

The ocean crashed again, louder than before.

"Are you coming to the house tonight?" Hattie asked, a little afraid of the answer.

"I think not."

"Father…."

"Better stay up here in the cold than be swept away making trips back and forth."

"We could rig a line."

"Nah, Hattie. Just bring me a blanket and a stout pot of coffee, and I will do well enough."

"I could stay with you," she offered hopefully.

"No, my dear. One can do it as easily as two, and I would rather have you tucked up in your bed."

"But I would rather—"

"Hattie, nothing is going to happen to me."

"I know." She gave a small sigh and put the rag down with the others. "I just can't sleep right knowing you're up the night in a chair, watching the lights."

"The storm's going to be a long 'un. You are just like old Pep, worrying if you can't have all your people under the same roof. There's no reason to worry."

Hattie chuckled. She remembered Pep, their old collie, whining and fretting all night when her oldest brother Chris was married and left the house.

Yes, she probably was a little like old Pep.

"All right, Father."

"There's a good girl." He leaned over and planted a kiss in her hair. His coat smelled of sea air and pipe tobacco. "You take the best care of me."

Thunder grumbled as she hastened down the stairs and out of the lighthouse.

Ten minutes later, as she headed back with two thick blankets and a piping hot pot of coffee, the rain started in fretful sheets. The black clouds that hung low over the wild sea crackled with lightning, and the waves that threw themselves upon the rocks reached further and further inland.

The wind howled dreadfully.

And then she saw it.

A dark head, raised above the murky water for a moment, then gone behind a swell. She stopped short, peering into the wild blue water. There it was again: a dark shape, fighting, but weakly.

A wreck. Hattie ran to the side of the house and rang the bell, slamming the clapper side to side with all her might. If anyone heard, there would be help within moments.

Gathering her skirts in one hand, she seized the coil of rope hung on the side of the house and ran out onto the rocky beach alone.

Her father was the first to answer the summons, running out after her, stumbling on the rocks. "Hattie, stop! Wait!"

The wind carried his words away as if he had whispered them.

The water fought her, throwing its weight against her as she staggered, not even knee deep, through its white spray. The rocks were slippery under her boots and the wind drove against her and around her, contrarily changing direction so she could not even brace against it before it changed. In seconds, the crashing spray and blurring rain had soaked her through.

"Sir, grab the rope!" Against the wind, her words were useless.

Determined, she gripped the coil in one cold hand, throwing it out as far as she could. She could feel but not hear the slap of the rope's end against the distant water. The waves caught it and dragged it, dancing like a boat on the end of an anchor, up and down the wild waves. But the dark head lifted again, closer now, and a pale hand reached out toward the rough rope.

Hope rose strong in her chest. "Grab it!" she shouted, the wind whisking her voice away.

A jerk on the other end nearly pulled her off her feet. He had the rope. A thought, brief and windblown, crossed her mind—what if she was not strong enough to bring him in herself?

But she couldn't spare an instant to fear, or to look back and see if help was coming. She threw her shoulder into the rope and started hauling as hard as she could. The man gained a half-foothold—she could feel through the rope when his feet struck ground. He fought forward, groping with hands and feet against the slick rocks.

She began to reach for him with one hand, but gave up, afraid of losing her grip on the rope. The sea was fighting for him, lashing her with blinding spray. Thunder cracked above them, threatening lightning.

Somewhere behind her a shout sounded. God be praised, someone was coming.

"Help me!" she shouted. A wave slammed her against the ground, filling her eyes and nose and mouth with salt water, but flinging the man within reach. She dug her fingers into the man's shirt and heaved, feeling her nails bend and then rip with the effort.

"Hattie!" Her father seized her around the waist to steady her, even as a wave crashed over them both, leaving foam streaming down them in its wake. Relief crept over her at the strength of her father's arms.

"He's so close!" she shouted, almost in her father's ear. Without a word he switched places with her, letting her brace him as he pulled hard on the man's shirt, then his arms, then his shoulders, finally gripping tight around his chest.

He threw up his head like a horse at a log pull. "We've got him! Heave!"

As Hattie started backward, a new voice sounded in her ear. "Behind you—hold steady!"

Mansell St. Jacques, their next-door neighbor, slipped in beside her.

"We have him, Hattie." The rain ran down her father's face and off his beard in streams. "Run ahead and get blankets and the kettle on. This man's as cold as ice!"

Hattie crammed her part of the rope into Mansell's large-knuckled hands and ran, glad the kettle was already hot. At a time like this, seconds mattered. Some men came in too cold and never warmed up.

She snatched up the abandoned blankets and the pot of coffee from beside the house where she had dropped them. The blankets were soaked. She unbolted the door and shoved it open with her shoulder, letting it swing wide, heedless of the deluge of rain that followed her.

A trunk stood beside the door for nights like this. Hattie threw open the lid, pulled out two thick, scratchy wool blankets, clutched them to her chest, and ran to the range, where she set the kettle to boil afresh. She opened the scraping metal front and gave the fire a stir. It rose at her bidding, blowing hot on her face.

"Hattie, my bed!" called her father.

She slammed the door on the range and ran to turn down the coverlet—her father's room was adjacent to the main room and closest at hand.

"Easy now," Mansell said as they laid the sailor down. "This leg's not right."

A faint moan came from the man, but he did not open his eyes. Her father bent over him, gently shifting the leg. A gash bled just above his knee.

Her father grimaced. "Nasty cut. We'll have to fetch the doctor."

"I'll see to that." Mansell straightened, his damp brown head almost brushing the ceiling. "Will you be all right?"

"Hattie is here." Her father looked up at her. "Get dry clothes. We have to get him out of these as quick as we can. And then get me coffee and whiskey."

The door slammed as Mansell left. The sea was muffled by the walls but roaring still, and in the sudden hush, Hattie could only think that her father had better get back to the lighthouse before the storm worsened.

She went to the dresser across the room and pulled out a stack of blankets, clean trousers, and a shirt. "Do you need any help?"

She laid the blankets and clothes down slowly on the end of the bed, and for the first time, she looked closely at the man.

He was rail-thin and pale, with black hair that hung just a tad longer than was respectable. His face was narrow and pointed at the chin; his fine nose jutted proudly like the prow of a ship. His clothes were ragged, torn from the rocks and the battering sea, but clearly not a seaman's clothes. The salt-stained shirt was long and tunic-like, high-collared and open past the collarbone, and it had once been black. Through a rip in one sleeve, Hattie saw an arm all blue above the elbow in a sickening criss-cross of bruises.

He was young.

Her father glanced up briefly. "Just get the coffee for him. I may have to cut off this trouser leg if the gash is too deep. I'll call you if I need help."

"Those are odd clothes he has on."

"Foreign," said her father, unfazed, unfastening the man's shirt. "It could be a ship has lost its way. Was there wreckage?"

"None that I saw."

A far-off alarm bell sounded in Hattie's mind. *No wreckage?*

"Thank you. Get me the shears first—I must get him out of these wet clothes."

Hattie produced the shears and returned to the kitchen, pulling down the cloudy-labeled bottle of medicinal whiskey from the cupboard.

As she poured a dash of it into a teacup full of coffee, her father's voice stopped her.

"Hattie, would you bring me some towels? Right away."

"Right away."

Hattie ran up the stairs, ignoring the sand and seawater she tracked up the freshly scrubbed wood. She brought several towels down to her father and stopped short beside the bed. Dark blood stained the sheets.

"How bad is it?" She held out a towel, averting her eyes from the wound. The man's wet shirt was gone and on his chest, fastened around his neck by a chain, lay a brass ring with a blue stone.

"We'll try these before we resort to a tourniquet." Her father's voice was grim. He took the towel and pressed it down on the man's leg, above the knee. Her father's hands were smeared with blood now.

The kettle across the room started to whistle, but no one moved. Thunder grumbled, closer than before.

"Another." Hattie silently handed over the second towel.

At last her father loosened his grip on the man's leg and checked it gingerly. "It's slowing, but I think it will need stitching. Get the kettle and fill those hot water bottles as fast as you can."

"Of course." Hattie hurried to the kitchen. A few minutes' work had the hot water bottles filled and wrapped in rags. She tucked them under the blanket beside and on top of the man, shuddering as her fingers brushed his cold, damp skin.

The wind hurled itself howling against house, rattling the windows. "Father, you should get back to the lighthouse."

Her father lifted the towel and grimaced again at the man's leg. "A few more minutes will not make much difference. When Mansell returns."

She swallowed her protest and went to fetch the coffee and whiskey.

The man's head lay back upon the pillow, every muscle in his face taut with pain. "I need you to drink this, sir." She slipped her arm under his neck and helped him lift his head just enough for her to set the rim to his mouth. His eyes opened briefly, just long enough to flicker to hers and then to the cup.

"There, easy." She glanced at her father, who was still pressing the towel against the wound. "You almost have it all down."

The man turned his head from the cup and began to cough violently. The cough caught and turned to retching, and a good deal of seawater and all the coffee poured out onto the bed and floor. Without a word, her father held out the extra towels.

A pounding started at the door.

Hattie left the mess and ran to open it.

She unbolted it to find Mansell carrying a flickering lantern, and with him was young Prins, the doctor's assistant.

"Doctor's running late." Regret tightened Mansell's rain-soaked face as he stomped in. "Lettie's having her twins."

"Lettie?" Her father's face lit up momentarily. Letitia was married to Jack, Hattie's second-oldest brother. She had been lying in for four weeks now, waiting.

"All's well so far," Mansell shrugged. Rainwater ran off his coat and onto the scrubbed floorboards. "But he won't be along for another hour at best."

Her father shook his head. "This leg needs stitching."

Mansell frowned. "Storm's getting worse. If you don't get out to the lighthouse now, Charles, you won't go at all. Prins and I will do it— I've stitched more in my day than a tailor. And Hattie is good help."

He glanced to Hattie, and she nodded briskly. "Go on, Father. We will be all right."

Her father gave a slight nod and handed the bandages over to Mansell, shutting the door firmly behind him.

The tall Frenchman paused halfway through shrugging off his coat. "You can do this?"

Hattie steeled herself against the vision of the blood-soaked sheets. "Yes, I've helped the doctor before."

"Good. Prins has chloroform to keep him subdued. Do you have supplies for surgery in that satchel, Prins?"

Prins nodded.

Mansell jerked his head toward Hattie. "She'll fix you up with boiling water. May as well get started."

Prins brought the bag to the kitchen table and began to organize an assortment of tools. He snapped the bag shut and went back to the bed. Hattie put the tools into a bowl and poured out the boiling water over them, but her eyes watched the two men through the doorway of her father's room as they examined the stranger's leg.

She heard Mansell growl in his throat. "Not pretty, is it?"

Prins had two fingers on the man's pale wrist. "Heartbeat's slow. Not dangerous yet, but heading that way. He's still powerful cold, too. What a mess—I don't think we can wait. Miss Scrow?"

She glanced down at the steaming bowl. "Just a minute more."

"That's good enough. Pull them out."

The tools were still hot to the touch when Hattie set them on her father's nightstand. Prins glanced up at Mansell, lowering his voice as though he were in church. "Do you really think we can do it?"

Mansell began to roll up his sleeves. "My stitching was the best of any man aboard the *Peggy Turner*."

"I haven't had to stitch anyone up yet," admitted Prins.

"I'll man the needle, then."

Prins bent over the man, administering a couple drops of chloroform on a rag. "Breathe slowly, now. Nice and deep." He turned to Mansell, speaking softly. "We'll still have to hold him down for the first few minutes. I don't think Miss Scrow wants that job." He glanced at Hattie. "Can you assist Mansell?"

She nodded.

The tall Frenchman looked down at her soberly. "You sure?"

For the space of a couple heartbeats the world was still, save for the flicker of the lamp against Mansell's long nose. The storm was a distant roar.

She swallowed. "Perfectly."

"Very well then." Mansell tilted his head to one side and pulled his mouth flat in an odd, grim smile. "Thread up the needle—it's now or never."

Hattie threaded the needle and handed it over.

He found her in the garden again, reading. The slip of a girl who could not train like the others, who kept to herself. Upon her lap was a book of ancient tales, worn by generations of use.

"You can come out," she said sweetly, looking up from her book. "You are many good things, but you are not quiet."

"What are you doing?" It was clear, of course, but he wanted to hear her say it.

"Reading the legends and prophecies." Her eyes were bright. "I love best the unfulfilled ones."

"Why?" He settled himself on the hot blue and white stones. "You can't know what happens."

"But that is exactly why I love them. What if they were about you, and you didn't know it?"

He studied a lizard skittering across the hot ground. "I hadn't thought of it like that."

She went back to reading.

"Do you—think any of them are about us?"

She smiled, and it was like sunshine. "Perhaps."

"Which?"

"I cannot say. If I do, perhaps they won't come true of us."

"Then how will we know?"

"We can't know for certain until it's over. The only thing you can do is make choices, one after another, and hope the fates smile upon us. No one becomes a hero, or a villain, without a choice. Everyone has a choice."

TWO

Sailor Boy

The house was silent except for the ticking of the clock on the mantel. The roaring storm had settled into a petulant squall, lashing rain against the windowpanes and growling at the door like a mad dog.

Hattie stirred the fire in the stove to life, fortifying it with wood from the kindling box by the side door. Mansell had gone home sometime in the thin, pale hours of the night, and her father still had not come in from minding the lights, so she was alone with the wounded man.

Images from the night before hovered in her mind. The lashing rain. The sailor. Mansell playing doctor. The man being sick, again and again, until the doctor had come and given him something strong to make him sleep.

She glanced at him through the open doorway of her father's room. His brows were knit and his nostrils flared as if with pain, even in his sleep. His black hair hung dry, but as straight as if it were still wet. He looked so thin and ill, that proud, troubled look sitting like a mask on his white face. Last night he had not moved an inch while Mansell cleaned the wound and stitched it up, though he had been at least half-conscious.

Hattie held her breath until she saw the steady rise and fall of the sheets over his chest. All was well.

She went to the pump and filled the kettle, taking care to be quiet. The pump did not wake him, nor the clank of the kettle on the stove, nor the scrape of the poker as she stirred the fire again. She glanced out at the fretful storm; her father would be in soon.

The clock struck seven in the hall.

The kettle began to mumble. With one more glance in the sailor's direction, Hattie fetched the teapot. Her father would want coffee with his breakfast, but what she needed right now was a cup of tea.

The kettle began to whistle softly as she measured her tea into the strainer. As the whistle grew more insistent, she picked up a towel and took the kettle off the range.

A thin groan broke the pleasant silence. The man was stirring, trying to sit up.

Hattie's spoon clattered to the floor.

"No, no, sir! You must not do that!"

He opened his eyes and looked into hers, making her stop short. They were strangely colored, shifting like the sea, and their expression was dangerous and wary, like a trapped animal.

Then the eyes softened. "It will not hurt me to sit up," he said gently, as if she was the one needing to be soothed. His English was good, but his accent was foreign, his voice wild as honey and dry as edge of a knife.

The sailor braced his hands against the bed and dragged himself up. In the effort, the wide neck of her father's half-buttoned shirt slipped off one shoulder.

The place on his arm that had looked like bruises the night before was glowing gently, marked in a deliberate pattern, like a tattoo, with a pale, unnatural blue.

Quick as the flick of a fish's tail, he pulled the shirt back over his shoulder. His hand crept to his neck, feeling for the chain. When he looked at her again, the wariness had returned to his eyes.

"Did I take hurt other than my leg?"

"No."

He pulled aside the coverlet and regarded the wound. "Hm."

"Twelve stitches," offered Hattie. "Does it hurt much? The doctor left—"

He stopped her with a brief wave of his hand. "I will need nothing for the pain. He did well, this friend of yours. It will not bleed much when I walk."

"But you're not—"

"I would be grateful if you could spare a sturdy cane or staff, and a coat. I wish that I could pay you for everything you have done, but I should delay no longer." Gritting his teeth, he moved his hurt leg from the bed to the ground.

Alarm rose in Hattie's chest, but she tried to speak firmly and calmly. "Oh, but you are going to stay. Until your leg is healed—it's no trouble at all."

He paused, considering the offer gravely. "I thank you for your kindness. But I think it best if I set on my way at once."

"It's storming out there, and it won't blow itself out for another day or two, my father says."

"That will be no trouble."

"But what could possibly be so urgent? We pulled you from the sea. If there was a wreck—"

She stopped, remembering the strange absence of wreckage.

She glanced again at the man, his dark hair falling over his wild-animal eyes and too-thin face, and thought of the hastily hidden tattoo. Suddenly she did not want to know. She had a sense, strange and distinct, that something was not right about this situation.

Perhaps he sensed her suspicion, for he moved his leg slowly back onto the bed. "In that case," he said cautiously, "I am glad to accept your hospitality. Perhaps you have some books I may read?"

Hattie shifted the worn volumes in her arm, pulling the top off the stack and setting it on her father's bedside table.

"*The Odyssey,* by Homer. *Tales of Faraway Places,* Tremaine. *Legends of the Ancients,* by…I cannot read the spine any longer." She gave an apologetic laugh. "And Lovelace."

The man moved Lovelace aside and picked up *Legends of the Ancients.*

"I didn't know what to bring you—I brought you some of my favorites, but if you would rather—"

He glanced up.

"These will do well. Thank you." He opened the cover gently and began to read down the table of contents.

"Would you like tea? I was about to make some. And breakfast— but you were very sick last night."

"Tea." A flicker of humor passed over his face "And too much seawater does tend to have that effect."

A key turned in the door and her father came in, shutting the door solidly against the storm.

"Good morning, Father!" Hattie threw him a smile. "Breakfast will be ready soon."

"Don't worry yourself, Hattie. How is our guest?" He peered into the open door of his bedroom and greeted the sailor with a nod. "Morning."

Their sailor raised his head from his book and returned the nod.

"Your color's returning. The doctor will be glad to see that when he comes this afternoon."

A cloud passed over the man's face. "There is no need."

"Nevertheless, he will come. Don't worry, no charge."

"I do not need it. And it is storming," he added, as though the thought had just occurred to him.

Hattie turned away to smother her smile. Their guest learned quickly.

"He's come out in worse weather than this. And he wants to keep an eye on that leg for a few days in case of infection."

This did not seem to sway the man. He thinned his lips grimly and returned to his book.

"Close as an oyster, that guest of yours." The doctor shut his satchel with a click. He picked the satchel up from the kitchen table and headed to the coat rack.

"Anything I should be concerned about?" Hattie could just catch her father's voice, lowered, speaking man to man.

"No, he's not dangerous—not that sort. But he's emaciated. There's evidence of past injuries. Rope burns on his wrists, old bruises, things he won't explain. That strange tattoo. And I suppose you heard no wrecks were reported yesterday?"

"I did."

"Just keep a weather eye out." He turned to Hattie, raising his voice. "And all the food he wants, hear? Looks like the ladies have been by already."

"Word travels fast." Hattie nearly laughed at the pies and covered dishes on the table. "Never fear. I'll do my best to put the meat back on his bones."

"I'm sure you will." The doctor's eyes crinkled in a smile. "Charles, good day." He put on his hat and went out into the blowing rain.

The stranger was looking about the room when Hattie brought his tea, his gaze resting particularly long on the window that faced the sea.

When he saw Hattie, he picked up Homer and began to flip pages.

"The doctor says you should eat." She set the tea down on the table beside him.

"Did he indeed?"

"There's all manner of food. Mrs. Goff brought by a feast from the ladies at the church—"

A gleam of wry amusement stole over his face. "The woman who lifted her eyes to heaven at the sight of me? I know what the word heathen means."

"She didn't mean anything by it, she's just—"

"I heard it. It was generous of you to excuse me as being ill, but I am not." He gritted his teeth as he shifted his position, then tossed the book listlessly.

"Do you not like Homer?" Hattie retrieved the book from the coverlet.

"No, I am very fond of him. I just—don't have the stomach for him at the moment."

"I suppose you've had enough of the sea just now."

A strange pang crossed his face. "No—I will never tire of the sea, nor fear it. But it puts me in mind of things I would forget if I could." He took a sip of his tea. "You enjoy the *Odyssey*, I take it."

He held the words out like a peace offering.

"Yes. I do."

"Don't you think it tragic? Ten years to get home, all the death and dying, all the delay?"

"Of course it's tragic. But the end is all the better for it." A spark of warmth started up inside her the thought. "It may have taken him ten years, but Odysseus came home to a wife who was faithful. Agamemnon couldn't say that, though the gods had not been set against his return."

He gave a small, bitter laugh.

"It's a better story than most the Greeks left us," she insisted. "It's a story of constancy."

"Sometimes I think Odysseus didn't deserve it. He brought many of his troubles on his own head."

"But that's exactly why I do like it." The warmth spread through Hattie, filling her voice with earnestness. "Who deserves anything? That didn't stop them from doing the right thing, and they were rewarded with a happy ending."

He gave a strange smile. "Isn't there a place for bearing what you have brought on yourself? Not every ending is happy."

Hattie thought that an odd thing to say.

THREE

At the Rim of the Dusky Sea

A growl of thunder rolled off the rocky coast, and out the window, Hattie saw a thin streak of lightning touch the restless horizon. Her father was by the door in his uniform, putting on his oiled coat.

She looked up from the pair of socks in her lap. "Will you want help minding the lights tonight, Father?"

"Oh, a mug of coffee when it's ready will be help enough." He knocked the ashes out of his pipe and opened the door.

Hattie smiled, looking down to make sure her stitches were even.

The sailor closed his book—the collection of ancient tales—and pulled himself out the armchair with an effort.

"Should—should you be getting up?" It had only been two days since his injury, and already he was spending most of his time in a chair, something the doctor had allowed reluctantly.

"I am not going far, Miss Scrow." He gave her a faintly amused look. He limped over to the table and poured himself a glass of Mrs. Goff's currant wine.

"Mind you don't," scolded Hattie pleasantly, setting down her darning. "I am going out, and there will be no one to help if you hurt yourself."

"That will not happen."

Hattie took down a tall mug and pulled the coffee pot off the stove. "It had best not."

The man gave her a thin smile and took a sip of his wine.

The thunder grumbled again as she thrust her arms into an oversized coat—left behind by one of her brothers—and went out after her father.

The night was restless and wild, the wind and the noise of the pebbles grinding underfoot drowning out lesser sounds. The faint light of Mansell's kitchen glowed beyond her in the thick darkness, and above her, like a mountain, towered the lighthouse, its beams thrust out into the night like the branches of an ancient pine.

It was the time of year when the sea was dark and restless and sorrowful, and tonight, against the warm golden light of the lamps, Hattie felt it keenly.

She opened the door and ducked into the lighthouse. "Shall I bring it up, Father?"

His voice echoed faintly down to her, though she knew he was shouting over the storm. "No need. Leave it down on the trunk."

She left the coffee and pushed the lighthouse door open against the pull of the wind. The sea roared on the rocks. She hastened her step toward the warm light of the cottage, then stopped short.

Their guest stood just outside the door, leaning against the brick wall, a heavy coat of her grandfather's draped over his shoulders. The light from the window played on the side of his grim face.

"What are you doing out here?"

He looked at her sideways.

"I'll leave you, then," she said, reaching for the door.

"No—" His voice stopped her. "I do not mind your presence. Unless the storm bothers you."

Hattie laughed. "Storms don't bother me."

"Then stay. Please."

She released the handle and leaned her back against the solid wood of the door. The wind pushed against them with renewed vigor. Lightning split the sky over the harbor like a crack in a pane of glass.

"It's something, isn't it?" Her voice was swallowed up by an answering peal of thunder.

He didn't answer, so she didn't volunteer anything more. She leaned against the door and felt very small in the face of the storm.

"Miss Scrow, are you afraid of me?" His voice broke the silence at long last.

"No." She looked up at him. "But you are hiding something. I know that."

He lifted his face to the wind. "I keep my secrets to protect those I care about."

"But when I asked the other day, you told me you had no one."

"No one you could contact with news of my well-being. There is a difference."

"And why could we not?"

He shifted, looking down at her. "For the same reasons I must keep the secrets." As he turned, that strange blue glow crept from the collar of his coat, illuminating his throat.

"You won't even tell me your real name."

At that, some of the stiffness left his stance. "It's Isurus—Lamnidae." With something of an effort, he held out his hand, which she shook. He dropped it as if he wasn't used to shaking hands. "I should have told you that before."

She didn't know what to say to that.

"I want you to know that I mean no one here any harm. You must forgive me if I keep my silence."

Something small twisted inside her, and she wanted to comfort him. "I didn't think you did."

"Then you are more trusting than I gave you credit for."

Hattie almost laughed. Her brothers had always teased that she was as suspicious as old Pep, growling at any sailor with a look in his eye she didn't like. "Oh, don't think I trust just anyone. I have seen enough in nineteen years."

"Then why do you trust me?" His expression was curious.

"Lies come quickly to bad men's lips. If you had bad designs, you would be less…lonely seeming."

"Less lonely," he echoed, his voice hollow, and turned his face to the rain.

Hattie pushed a strand of hair out of her face and turned the handle on the glass-paned front door of the general store. The bell rang cheerfully as she pushed it with her basket and shut the door firmly behind her.

Matthew Starbuck glanced up from his book—D'Aubigné's *History of the Great Reformation* today—and moved his glasses onto his nose to see her. "Well, good morning, Miss Scrow. How is your father?"

"He is well, thank you, except for the strain in his back."

"And I suppose he's down a hand, with you taking care of the invalid."

"The invalid practically takes care of himself," Hattie laughed. "And the doctor has been over nearly every day." She stepped over a snoring dog to reach a tin of baking soda. "The Ladies' Aid society has been bringing more meals than we can eat. I had to send Fred home with a whole pot of chowder and a cherry pie yesterday. I daresay Margaret will scold me for tempting him with so much pie."

"Your brother needs it, hard as he works out there. This break in the weather won't last long."

"Yes." Hattie's gaze strayed out the window to the bay, which was little more than a blurred line of dark blue, obscured by the boats and shacks that lined the wharf.

"So what is it you need?"

"Just soda and lard." Hattie paused to look at a bottle of vanilla on the shelf.

"That's straight from Madagascar, that is," said Starbuck. "Finest there is."

Hattie turned it wistfully on the shelf. It thrilled her to think how far away Madagascar was. But she couldn't afford it.

She shrugged and moved on. "Maybe one day."

"What are the biscuits for?"

"Supper. Our guest does not know what biscuits are, so I'm making some to go with Mrs. Gardener's stew tonight."

"How is he?"

"Improving quickly. His leg will take some healing, but I daresay he will be off to wherever he came from soon enough."

"What ship was he from again?"

Hattie became occupied in studying a bundle of dried lavender hanging from the rafters. "He didn't say."

"Word around town is he's a bit mad," offered Starbuck conversationally.

Hattie's lips tightened a little. "He does not seem to be mad. Foreign, yes."

"Well, so says Mrs. Huddleston. She says he has pagan symbols drawn all over his skin and wild eyes. 'Mad as a march hare,' said she."

"People will talk," said Hattie amiably but firmly. "But there's rarely anything to it. How much do I owe you?"

The house was still, still as the warm sunshine casting the patterns of the windowpanes upon the floor. Isurus was not there.

Hattie set her shopping basket on the kitchen table. Strange, that the house was empty and she had not seen him on the paths or down by the water.

She unpacked the basket, glancing out at the sea as she did. It was dark and restless, but cracks of blue sky showed on the cloudy horizon.

A creak on the back porch arrested her attention. The door swung open with a rattling of glass panes and her brother Fred, closest to her in age, came striding through. His chestnut hair resembled windblown sea-grass, and his blue eyes sparkled with mischief.

"Afternoon, Hattie-girl!" He planted a kiss on her cheek. "How is the old lighthouse?"

"It's well." She threw her arms around him in a hug. He always smelled of salt air and fish.

"Where's that sailor? I thought he was staying here."

"He's somewhere, and I'm not quite sure he's a sailor."

"Really? So all that gossip in town is true?"

"Not all of it." Hattie put the lard away with a wry smile.

"Look, Hat, I only have a minute, but I cannot find my Lovelace anywhere. I thought I took it with me before the wedding, but Margaret says she hasn't seen it at all, so perhaps I left it here?"

"Anything you left would be in the attic now, with Father's books."

"I don't suppose you could look for it when you get a chance? I'd do it myself, but I promised Margaret I'd be home by quarter past."

Quarter past. A glance at the old clock on the hearth proved he was already running late.

"Are you on your way home?"

"Yes, why?" He paused in the doorway.

"Take another pie?"

"Couldn't possibly. Margaret would kill me. We're still finishing the one you gave me yesterday." He flashed a grin and made his escape.

"If you say so," Hattie replied to the empty space he left behind.

The attic was something of a refuge for her father—after her mother died, he'd made one end of it into a study with a desk and his collection of books and journals and atlases. When Hattie was young, she had spent hours upon hours pressing flowers on rainy days among the poems and Greek legends. It had been her favorite place in the house.

Even the familiar musty smell that greeted her as she opened the door to the stairway and mounted the steps made her feel young and hopeful again.

Isurus was sitting at her father's desk, poring over the largest atlas.

"Excuse me." Seeing her, he started to his feet.

"No, no—don't stand."

He settled back into his chair, wincing slightly, but did not relax. "I did not wish to take your father's bed and chair any longer, so he directed me to a room upstairs—and here, where the books are."

"I see. Well, I am just after a volume of poetry. My brother thinks he left it here."

"You have a brother?" Something changed in Isurus's face—whether for good or bad, she could not say.

"Three of them. All older, married now. My brother Fred only this summer. I miss him the most."

"I am sure. What is the volume?" He seemed eager to change the subject.

"Lovelace. The poet. Have you read him?"

"I have now, since you loaned him to me."

"Oh." How stupid of her. She had given the book to Isurus. "Well…I am sure Fred can wait, if you want it longer."

"No need." Isurus seemed to comprehend her distress. "I am finished with it."

Her curiosity overcame her embarrassment. "Did you like it?"

"He has a gentle way of expressing himself. A kind of fine longing in his words…particularly, I think, when he writes poems to Lucasta."

Hattie nodded, suddenly awkward. She turned to the books on the shelves, running her fingers over the spines.

"Your father has many interesting books. Strange ones too."

"My father was good friends with an explorer. I think he rather wanted to be one himself, once. We have some of his friend's journals…he died of a disease he contracted in Brazil, but he traveled all over the world."

"What did he do in his travels?"

"Mostly he looked for ancient ruins. Aztecs, Egyptians. He was even chosen by someone in England for an expedition that was to search for Atlantis somewhere off the coast of Spain, but they couldn't fund the vessel. He always regretted that."

Isurus cleared his throat. "I will get Lovelace." He rose slowly.

"You needn't, I can get it."

"I would rather. I will return to this later."

She stood gazing aimlessly at the books on the shelf as she listened to his slow footsteps retreating down the stairs. It was silly for him to go with his hurt leg when she was there, but she had the keen feeling that he wanted to get away from her.

So she waited.

On the desk where Isurus had been sitting was her father's atlas, opened to the islands of the Aegean and Ionian seas.

Beside the atlas lay *Legends of the Ancients* and one of the travel journals, full of rough sketches, translations of old Latin and Greek inscriptions, and a drawing of ring with a blue stone. Something about it plucked at the edge of her memory.

She picked up *Legends of the Ancients*, pleased that he had enjoyed it enough to bring it with him. It had been a favorite of hers and Fred's when they were younger.

He had bookmarked his place with a scrap of paper, and smiling, she opened the place. *Atlantis, Myth or History?*, the chapter heading asked boldly.

The paper was marked with numbers in handwriting she didn't recognize, latitude and longitude.

Instinctively, she ran her fingers over the rigid lines of the map, looking up and down, side to side. The latitude and longitude were there—over a blank section of sea.

The feeling that something was not quite right came over her like clouds over the sun, and she shut the book, quickly.

The wind pressed against the white-paned windows, making them creak. The kettle hissed over the fire; the smell of fresh bread filled the small house.

"Miss Scrow?"

Hattie set down the tea tin and looked up.

"I should like to go down to the sea."

"Are you sure you should? The wind is strong, and your leg is not."

"It has been nearly a week, and I am as restless as a caged shark. My leg will not strengthen without use. If you lend me a cane, I will do well enough."

"But your stitches?"

He smiled. "Miss Scrow, I think you greatly underestimate me."

Hattie smoothed her apron and crossed the room. "I have my grandfather's old cane somewhere." She rifled through the umbrella stand and after a few moments pulled out a gold-headed cane. "Will this do?"

"It will." Isurus stood and limped over to her.

"Isurus—I have to say, I am not sure going out by those rocks is the best idea."

Isurus reached for the cane. "Well, you are honest. I have done worse in my day; let me be a fool if I want."

Hattie retained her grip on the cane. "One misstep on those rocks and that wound could open up again."

His voice was gentle, almost mocking. "You think *I* would slip?" For a moment, a fierce, faraway look lit in his eyes. Then he quenched it. "I have done many things, Miss Scrow, but I have never slipped."

He moved past Hattie, leaning heavily on the cane, and went out into the wind.

Hattie stood in the doorway, drinking in the gray sky, unable to bring herself to shut the door with Isurus out on his own. The wind played with her wide skirt, whisking it against the door frame like the pennant on a brig. Fall was coming on, with all the promise of brisk storms and thundering nights.

Isurus made his way slowly down the spit of sand and pebbles to the shore, where the sea washed restlessly against rocks and cold sand. He cut a strange figure—tall, bent over an old man's cane, his face young and proud under his unkempt black hair. He looked like an old hero from an ancient legend, silhouetted against the fretful sea.

The thought made her uneasy.

She took her shawl down from the peg by the door and went out after him.

He was walking steadily when she gained his side, but she could see sweat slicking his neck. "I hope you didn't come all the way out here just to keep an eye on me."

Hattie clasped her hands behind her back. "I like the sea when it's like this."

Isurus gave her a reproachful smile.

"And yes, I came out to keep an eye on you."

He shrugged. "Then you may watch me. But you will find your time wasted."

They continued on in silence, listening to the roar of the waves and the grinding of the pebbles under their feet.

The sea crashed hard against the shore, and Isurus's face darkened. "I do wonder if Odysseus regretted again and again that he left his home for a foreign war."

"I suppose he thought about it." Hattie brushed stray hair out of her eyes. The sea spray was flying on the brisk wind, dampening everything. "But, after all, he was forced to go. It was not as if it was his fault." She pulled her shawl tighter around her shoulders as the wind snatched at it.

He clenched his fist tightly. "Odysseus could have tried harder."

"And how would you know?"

"Twenty years he was gone. When you have a home that calls out to you more strongly than a siren, and the strain pulls your heart out of your chest every waking moment—I know that he could have."

Isurus lifted a handful of sand and pebbles, dripping saltwater. "What an exile this is," he whispered. The wind brought the ghost of the words to her ears, otherwise she never would have heard them.

He was stranger than usual today, so stark and lonely.

"There is nothing that can help this," he said grimly. "Here I am, like Odysseus, an exile at the rim of the dusky sea, waiting for my redemption."

The sea only crashed against the rocks in reply.

"An exile?"

His mouth thinned to a hard line. "Do not repeat that."

"All right. I wouldn't have anyway."

"Word has a way of getting about your town, I have noticed."

"Certainly not through me." Hattie lifted her chin stubbornly. "I abhor gossip."

"I am glad to hear it. You would seem to be an exception in this lonely place."

"Our people have faults, like all of humankind. But we are loyal and tough and fight the sea for a living. There's a lot of merit in that."

Something softened in Isurus's face. He lowered himself onto a broad, dark rock beside the water, and the movement caused the chain with the ring to slip out and swing against his chest.

He fingered it lovingly a moment before shoving it back inside his shirt.

"That's a fine ring," commented Hattie, simply looking for something to say.

The moment she said it, the sketch of the ring in the attic

flashed into her mind.

"It was my father's." Isurus looked up at her, his eyes the color of the murky sea. Then his voice hardened. "But he's dead."

He fingered a rock that lay beside him and threw it hard into the windblown sea.

"It's strange…it looks like a sketch I saw in one of the journals upstairs."

Isurus's face darkened. Mentioning it had been a mistake.

"You saw that, did you?" was all he said.

In the depths of the pool the great shark moved, each turn of his powerful tail smooth and lazy. The boy dipped his hand into the water, letting it run over his fingers, imagining that he could touch the rough, cool skin. It seemed like mere inches separating him from the shark, but it was three or four fathoms down in the clear water.

"What are you doing?"

His shoulders relaxed at the sound of her voice. Given the choice, he would rather be greeted by his brother and companions, but this girl—her presence was comfortable, like the warm sun on his back.

"Watching Tareth. He is the king of all sharks. None is his equal."

"He is not," she said, her voice equal parts chiding and reverent. "Moraire is."

"She's a terror." A shiver ran cold beneath his warm, smooth skin.

"She's the Fate. Untamable."

"I don't like things that cannot be tamed. What if she turned against you?"

"There is nothing admirable about being tamed." The girl dipping her bare toes in the clear water above Tareth. "Untamable means that you have power that no one can take away from you."

She shoved her thick hair back over her small shoulder. "The man who settles for things that can be tamed—he is a fool and weakling. But power…."

She kicked a spray of water into the air and it became a hundred diamonds, hung on beams of sunlight. "If it cannot be taken away, what's to separate you from the gods?"

FOUR

A Sprig of Rosemary

The first star of the night was a pinprick of silver in the soft blue sky, blurred by the steam that rose from the pit in the pebbly sand. The smell of salt and steaming seaweed mingled with the aroma of fresh corn and steamed clams, the clatter of plates as her sisters-in-law laid everything out on the table, the laughter of her brothers filling the cool evening air.

Hattie closed her eyes and took it in.

Every year, since she was almost too small to remember, they had done this—even after her mother died.

Her father was crouched on the sand, checking the food gingerly with a stick.

"Almost ready," he announced, straightening with a groan. "What say you, Hattie? Are you ready?"

She grinned broadly. "I was ready an hour ago."

"Hear that, Chris? Hat was ready an hour ago," echoed Jack, her middle brother, the tall one in the family.

"That's the secret. Hattie's the eater in the family." Chris bestowed this information upon Isurus quite solemnly. Fred, standing beside him, burst into laughter.

Isurus gave a small, polite nod. He already stood out like a pine tree in an orchard, dark and solemn compared to her brothers with their chestnut hair and loud laughter. Hattie wondered if he was enjoying himself at all.

He still bore a faint limp, but he had taken a job with Sackett, a local fisherman, who was down a hand for the season.

Hattie was glad he had taken the job. Why she wanted him to stay, she didn't know; he seemed to carry a cloud with him wherever he went. But she was glad all the same.

"Fred, come over here and give me a hand with the table!" A woman's voice—Margaret's—rang across the beach in the direction of the firepit, where the men stood with their arms folded.

The tangle of brothers separated, and Fred ran off to help.

Chris crouched down beside their father to consult about the readiness of the crabs, and Isurus and Jack began to talk, staring out at the water.

The wind carried the fresh, familiar smell of the steaming clams to her. A laugh burst out—Jack's—but she saw that Isurus was smiling, actually smiling. It made his thin face suddenly pleasant and real, nothing like the constant marble expression he wore.

Her father rose up, letting out a seaman's bellow. "Supper is ready!"

By the time dinner was finished and the cleaning up had commenced, the daylight was a whisper of light above the thick Maine treeline. Lanterns glowed outside the cottage, and Fred was building up the fire while her father checked the lights.

The other women were in the house, and through the windows Hattie could hear the merry clank of dishes in the sink and snatches of happy conversation.

She grasped the tablecloth and gave it a firm shake onto the sand.

"Need help?" Chris came over, taking the other end of the cloth.

"I won't say no," replied Hattie, beginning the fold.

"I say." Her brother checked his ends with the deliberation of one unused to folding tablecloths. "How well do you know this man staying with you?"

"A bit, but he's quiet. Why?"

"Well, Rob Sackett and I were sharing the water out past the bay, maybe two, three days ago. One of his men raised a shark on accident. Young four-footer. It was wild—I could see it thrashing about—and then this fellow," —he gave a nod in the direction of Isurus, who was observing the building of the fire—"he went right to it."

"And?"

"Well, that's the thing. I've never seen anything like it in my life. He put his hand right on it, and it settled like a horse. He was talking to it, too. Sackett said whatever it was, it certainly wasn't English. And then he pressed his forehead against it—I saw it with my own two eyes—and put it back in the water."

"That's strange." She held the folded tablecloth against her chest. Why was her heart beating faster than it should?

"It wasn't just strange, Hattie. I wish you could have seen it, it was—it wasn't natural." Chris scratched the back of his head wryly. "We've been around the sea our whole lives, Hat. We've worked in it and fought it, and I can point you out a sailor from a mile away. But that man, Isurus—it's like he knows it in a different way than any of us."

Isurus was standing, a little obscured by the smoke, watching the horizon solemnly.

"And why are you telling me this?"

"Sackett wanted to know if I knew anything. I said you'd know, if anyone did, since he's been staying here."

"He hasn't said anything."

The maps and the ring came to her mind, but she thrust the thought away. What would she tell Chris? That Isurus had been looking at maps and journals? Out loud, it seemed inconsequential.

She took the tablecloth up to the house.

The fire was crackling and spitting over the damp sand, sending slick, hot air up into the cool night sky. The stars were coming out in earnest.

She settled on the ground in front of the fire, drawing her knees up under her long skirt and leaning her arms across them, watching the family as it now was—Fred splashing water at Margaret, Jack proudly showing the twins off to anyone who would look, her father and Chris talking about the coming weather.

"What is it?" Isurus lowered himself onto the sand beside her.

"Nothing." She ducked her head away slightly. After what Chris had said, she felt a little shy in Isurus's presence.

"Nothing I did?"

"No." Hattie leaned her chin against her wrists. "It's just this—this is what life is, and I love it with all my heart."

Isurus chuckled low in his throat, a warm sound.

"And I think, especially on beautiful nights like this, how I want nothing to change. I just want it to go on and on this way forever."

General laughter rose over the crackle of the fire.

"But life has to change, doesn't it?"

"Yes." Perhaps it was her imagination, but Hattie sensed a note of bitterness. She looked over at him and his face was marble again.

"And it does not always change for the better. You cannot choose what life does to you." Isurus looked down the beach at her family. "But this—what your family has—" He sighed. "I have seen the pinnacle of riches and power, and this has it beaten by a fathom and more."

Hattie did not know whether she was more surprised by the talk of riches or by his slipping into local speech. She smiled wryly, trying to cover her discomfiture with a joke. "I don't know. You've met my brothers."

"Quite a set of them, you have."

Letitia took one of the twins from Jack's arms as it began to wail. He was grinning sheepishly. A month or more, and he still grinned like a fool at the sound of the babies.

"They're more sensible when they are apart."

"There are worse things than enjoying each other's company." The marble mask was gone, but he was deeply in earnest. "It is a good thing, to have loyalty and love for one's family."

Something in his voice failed.

A reply was on Hattie's tongue when Fred dashed over, damp and laughing.

"Hattie, tell Jack to get off me!"

"What did you do?" Hattie made no move to get up and defend him.

"He splashed the baby!" Jack came running up the beach, depositing the baby in Hattie's arms and making a sudden snatch at Fred.

"It's Lettie you are going to have to run from." Chris was watching the scene with quiet amusement.

As the baby wasn't even crying, it couldn't have been more than a few drops. Hattie tucked the blanket around the baby's tiny, grasping hand.

"Do you have a brother?" Jack asked over his shoulder, his eyes on his quarry. Fred was backing away, laughing.

Isurus looked on with amusement. "One." The admission seemed to come easily.

"Then surely you understand how maddening they are." Jack seized Fred by the collar. "Sometimes you just want to throw them into the sea."

"Naturally." The words came in the same light tone.

If Hattie hadn't glanced at him just then, she wouldn't have seen the strange, white look on his face. As if he had just watched someone die.

He left the day he told her about Atlantis.

Hattie was finishing the garden, cleaning out the last of the tomato plants. Only the herbs and the pumpkins were left, visible now that their vines were dying.

Isurus came out of the cottage, the few things he could call his own slung in a bag over his shoulder.

Hattie had known this time would be coming, but somehow, seeing him stride out across the grass toward town, it struck her harder than she had expected.

He paused at the end of the garden, plucking a sprig of rosemary, turning it in his fingers as if it were a jewel.

"Isurus, are you leaving us?"

He looked up quickly.

"I did not see you, Miss Scrow." He strode to her through the garden. "Yes, I am taking my leave."

A slow ache began in her throat. "I thought you were staying on with Sackett for the season."

"Oh—" Understanding dawned on his face. "I am. He has offered me a room, and I thought it no longer right that I should stay in your home. You and your father have already been more than good to me."

"It was our pleasure." She dropped her eyes from his face and saw the rosemary, still held between his fingers. "What's that?"

"Oh, it's rosemary—for remembrance." He made a quiet, apologetic noise in his throat. "When I go home, it will be a reminder to me."

"So you do have a home."

Isurus nodded, glancing away. "You may think I am a fool. To you, perhaps, it makes no sense that I should refuse to speak of such things and remain here so long while I have a home, but—"

"I don't think you are a fool."

"The truth is," he stumbled on quickly, "there are many reasons why, as of yet—I cannot tell anyone at home that I live. For your protection, partly. If they knew, they would send someone to kill me, perhaps to kill you and your father for aiding me."

Hattie bit her lip. The world had grown very close and still.

"Perhaps I should not have told you that."

"No. It's hard for someone to bear such heavy secrets alone."

"It's my duty." He swallowed. "You'd be surprised how much easier it is when you care about those you protect. For I must protect those I left behind as well."

"What from?"

His mouth twitched, and he pressed the back of his hand briefly against it.

"We are a proud and secretive people. To be discovered—to be the one through whom my homeland is discovered—would be a dishonor I could not outlive. And when I washed up here, I had to know that no one was going to spread my secret."

"You do not have to tell me." She reached out as if to comfort him but did not touch him. "I don't need an explanation. I understand."

"No, I think I want to tell you. Your family saved me, and to you, I want to give the truth."

Hattie waited quietly.

"I am from Atlantis. I was born to a—a high family. Upon my father's death this spring, my brother, my own brother, had me accused of a crime I did not commit." He looked away from her as if he hadn't the strength to go on otherwise. "He had me executed so that he could have my inheritance."

It was silent between them.

Hattie studied the dirt on her fingers; she was acutely aware of the dirt, but there was a warmth growing inside her that she could not quite explain.

Isurus's hand closed over his bag again, as if he was resolving again to leave.

"But you didn't die."

"What?"

Hattie looked up at him with a small smile. "You didn't die. He failed. You're going back to take it away from him, I hope."

He breathed in softly. "Well, yes."

"Good." The wind off the sea picked up, brisk and insistent.

"Well." He cleared his throat. "I am going to be late, I fear. Do tell your father what I told you. I think he would be pleased—about Atlantis."

"He will, I know it." Hattie held out her hand, dirt and all.

"Farewell, Isurus, and God be with you."

He hesitated. "I do hope that I will see you in town, now and again? That is, if you wish it."

Hattie nodded, her smile growing. "I do."

"Until next time, then." He took her hand gently and kissed it.

There was something wistful in that kiss.

FIVE

The Sea Takes

"Going out so early?"

Sun streamed through the window, but Hattie's father was headed to bed. It had been a rough night with the lamps.

She shifted the basket on her arm. "Yes, I thought I'd get out of your way this morning. You can sleep, I will do the shopping, and when I am back, you will have gotten some rest."

"It's quiet with that Isurus fellow gone." Her father stretched his stiff arms. "I rather liked him."

"I did too."

Hattie gripped the basket tighter, pushed the door open, and strode out into the warm sun.

The beach was strewn with odds and ends, wood and string and dead fish and long-empty shells. A few pine branches decorated the sand and pebbles around the cottage, showing the ferocity of the night's weather.

But today—today was cool and full of sunshine.

She started down the wharf, humming to herself, enjoying the light breeze that played with the loose ends of her hair. The wharf was the lifeblood of the town, and it was humming this morning, sailors and fishermen casting loose and heading out, others rowing about with boats already full of fish.

Craning her neck, she could see Isurus at work, his face solemn but pleasant as he readied the nets with the rest of Sackett's hands.

She smiled and walked on.

"Morning, Miss Scrow!" greeted Starbuck, as she entered into the general store to the jangle of the bell.

"Good morning, Mr. Starbuck." She ducked under the hanging onions and lavender and paused beside the shelf of spices. The Madagascar vanilla was still there.

"I see you're still admiring that," commented Starbuck.

"Yes." She held it a long moment, then put it back with a little smile. "Someday."

Next was the butcher's, which still had an old-fashioned hanging wooden sign with a black and white pig, freshly painted. Mr. O'Toole greeted her cheerily as she stepped into his shop.

"Top of the mornin', pretty lass!" He put down his cleaver with a slam and came over. "What can I get ye?"

"A cut of beef, a quarter of lamb. How's business?"

"About like it always is, Miss Scrow." He unwrapped the paper with a smile. "Hey Pat, get me a quarter of lamb, will ye?"

O'Toole slapped down the cut of beef and began wrapping it with his big hands. "I've heard your sailor's a hard worker."

"Of course he is." It unsettled her to hear him call Isurus "her sailor," though she knew perfectly well what he meant.

"Works like a dog at the docks, has a clean mouth and the best mind for figures Sackett's ever seen. Wish we could find where he came from and get more like him." He winked. "But he's leaving come winter, isn't he?"

"So I understand. When he's saved up passage to wherever he's going."

"Pity. It's the good ones that leave."

Patrick came out of the back with a quarter of lamb, and O'Toole wrapped it quickly.

"There you go, miss. And wish your father a good day from me."

"I will!" The weight of the basket pressed into her arm as she packed the meat away.

As she made her way through the street and back toward the wharf, a voice called her name.

She turned and saw Isurus leaning against a lamppost, his hands shoved in the pockets of his coat.

"Good morning, Isurus."

He stirred with a small smile and pushed himself off the lamppost. "Why, good morning, Miss Scrow." He fell into step beside her. "Where are you going this morning?"

"Down to the wharf, now. I am going to pick up some fresh herring."

"For supper?"

"Yes. I buy them from Mansell. And what are you doing?"

"I just saw you in town and thought I might say good morning, ask how your father is."

"He's well. But why aren't you down at the docks?"

"Mr. Sackett has already cast off. I just have to mend his nets and traps while he is out and run up some figures."

"So you've been beached."

"Just for today. He found out that I could do figures, and he needed last week's catches tallied."

Hattie smiled appreciatively.

"I should get back to the nets soon, but I saw you and thought I could spare a moment to go to the general store and to say good morning."

"Oh, I've already been to the general store," she said, regretting it a little.

"I see." He glanced in her basket. "Are you baking?"

"Yes, I'm making cookies for Jack. Tomorrow's his birthday."

"He is a lucky brother." Isurus stopped in the road and turned to look at her. "I saw you in the store, actually. I noticed you looked at that dark bottle on the shelf for a long time before you put it back."

"You were watching me?"

His brow creased slightly. "Not like that, Miss Scrow."

She shook her head, smiling. "Well, it was nothing. Just vanilla. I can't afford to spend money that way unless it is a very special occasion."

"I see." Isurus resumed walking, his face solemn, and Hattie fell in step beside him.

"One day I will. On a very special day."

"One in particular?"

"No, not that I know of yet."

"We have a saying where I come from: The heart chooses which day the sun shines brightest." He reached into his pocket and drew out a small, paper-wrapped package.

"Isurus, you did not!" Hattie stepped back, torn between delight and dismay. "You can't spend your money like that, and not on me. Did you not say that you were saving money to leave?"

He gravely held out the package again. "Please take it."

She reached out hesitantly. "But you must let me pay you."

"No, no!" He shook his head vehemently. "It is a gift."

"A gift…."

"Yes." He waited, it seemed to Hattie, holding his breath.

She tucked the vanilla into her basket. "Thank you." Her heart was singing, but her thrifty mind still could not reconcile the sacrifice. "But whatever did you go and do that for?"

He shrugged. "I wanted to. You seemed so fond of it, and it

seemed a small price to pay if it made you happy."

"Well, it did." The pleasure in his face warmed her and made her awkward at the same time. "I mean, it—thank you. I'll think of you every time I use it."

She didn't say *after you're gone,* but they were both thinking it.

Isurus thrust his hands in his pockets and strode away.

"Hattie!" Her father came through the front door, bringing with him a strong gust of wind and evening air.

A storm was rolling in—the sort the town braced for, tying up boats and locking away nets and traps. In town, the women would be preparing food and hot water bottles, a few hardy fellows would be staking out places to watch for vessels returning from the sea, and somewhere, somehow, Isurus would be in the middle of it all.

The lights were needed more than ever on a night like this. Her father would be out in the cold all night; he could be scraping ice off the lighthouse windows before morning.

Uneasiness settled in her stomach. "How are the lights? Will you need help?"

"No. They're burning like champs. But I just got word from town. There's talk of a floundering ship." Her father sat heavily in the armchair and pulled off his boots.

"Coming here?"

"Mr. Winters and Mr. Sackett went out to aid with the rescue. They won't make it to any harbor, so I hear from the report."

Hattie let her breath out slowly. If Mr. Winters had gone, Fred had probably gone with him.

"Is there something you can take down to the church? They'll be gathering food for the survivors."

"I have a chicken pie and an apple—I was making them for you tonight."

"Take them. From the way they spoke, it probably won't be long before they arrive. Unless, God forbid, we lose our men as well."

Hattie glanced out at the wild sea. "They will be back."

She went to the door and took her coat down from its peg.

"Would you like something warm to drink?"

"No, I can get it myself, dearest. Just take your pies down there before the weather gets worse."

"I will save you some." She walked over and kissed his cheek. "Just you wait and see."

"Don't bother. I'll be right as rain with bread and cheese."

Hattie put the pies in a basket and buttoned up her coat. "Be careful, Father."

"I'll rig a line, don't you worry. And Hattie, if the weather's bad, don't come back right away. I'll be fine here."

"All right."

She hated leaving him with the weather so unpredictable. One turn of the wind as he went from tower to cottage, and he could be swept away.

But she wouldn't let herself think of that.

The wharf was empty except for a few brave men watching the water, but she could see people going in and out of the church hall. The houses on the waterfront were lit, people watching and waiting as darkness fell, ready to move into action at a moment's notice.

She was greeted at the doors of the church by Ruth Hutchison, a young mother of four children. "Evening, Hattie! You've come through again."

"It's just pie." Hattie handed it off to two eager eleven-year-olds. "Any news?"

"None yet," said Mrs. Goff from the corner, where she was shaking dust out of a stack of blankets. "But our best boys are watching."

Mrs. Sackett, standing by the door, gave a smile that seemed a little strained.

"Rob Sackett and Ian Winters are the two best seamen in Roke Point," came a loudly expressed opinion from the kitchen. "There's not an ounce of worry should be wasted on them. They'll save those poor souls, they will."

Shouts rose outside. "Survivors!" Young Timothy Granger came bursting in. "Sackett's boat is back full—there must be thirty or more!"

The room moved almost as one. Many of the women streamed out to see and to help, and the rest began setting out food.

Hattie had not even had a chance to pull off her coat. She turned and ran out onto the steps. Men were already approaching from the wharf in huddling, stumbling groups.

She saw Isurus, tall and straight in his heavy coat, a limping man's arm thrown over his shoulder.

She ducked back into the church hall. "They're coming. It's going to be a crew."

"Quick then, help me ladle up this soup. It's going to go faster than cakes at a state fair."

Hattie took up a station behind a table and began to ladle out beef stew and hot chowder with a will. The soaked and weary sailors streamed in, taking the soup and coffee and blankets eagerly, but retaining the orderly manner of men who are grateful to be alive.

Isurus helped his man into a chair beside Prins and spoke with him a moment. Then he crossed the room and got two cups of coffee.

He caught Hattie's eye from across the room and smiled the faintest of smiles.

After the first rush of sailors came through, Hattie left the soup and went to help with the first aid. Most of the hurts were scrapes and bruises, things easily dealt with by anyone with witch hazel or warm water and a bandage. One man, an older fellow with a sweet smile minus a couple teeth, had a skinned arm, which she washed and wrapped.

"You're a mighty fine lass to be spending a cruel evening patching up old fellows like me," he said, grinning sheepishly.

"Nonsense. When there is a storm, we pull together. Now go on, and eat your fill of warm food."

"Oh, I have. Your town sure knows how to cook a feast."

He moved on, and Hattie glanced around. No one seemed to be waiting.

"Miss Scrow?" Isurus came over, dragging the empty chair closer with his foot. He held out a pair of badly scraped hands.

"Isurus, what did you do?"

"I did it when we were tying up the boats. A couple of them pitched away."

Hattie clucked her tongue and turned to get the witch hazel. "How are you going to work tomorrow?"

"I can still use them." He sounded amused.

Hattie shook her head. "But should you?" She took his left hand first and gently laid the damp cloth over the bloody scrape.

"You needn't, Miss Scrow."

"Needn't what?"

"Make a fuss over me."

Hattie could not quite meet his gaze as she pulled the cloth off and reached for the warm water.

"Miss Scrow?"

"Isurus—" She raised her eyes to his. "I think you may call me Hattie sometimes, when it is just us."

"Perhaps that day will come."

"But not yet?" She wrung the cloth out and reached for the bandage.

"Not quite yet."

Hattie wound the bandage around his hand, tying it off. "Are you going home now?"

"No." He got slowly to his feet. "They may need help yet."

The doors opened and Fred slipped in, followed by a gust of icy wind. "Fred!" Hattie ran to him, throwing her arms around his neck. "You made it in!"

Fred shook his head. "No, Winters hasn't come in yet. We're still waiting on him."

"Oh. I thought you would have gone." Relief rose in her chest, along with a whisper of fear. Sackett's men had come in nearly forty minutes ago.

"I was off closing up the boathouse when word came. Jack was at the wharf…he went instead."

"I see." Hattie swallowed back a sick feeling.

But Jack was strong and sea-wise. If anyone could make it back, it was Winters and Jack.

Fred gave her a squeeze. "Go help. Don't think about it. I'm getting soup and then going back out to watch."

"Of course." Hattie forced a smile.

Worrying never did a mite of good.

She went into the kitchen where Mrs. Goff and Mrs. Hutchison were cleaning and minding a pot of soup. Two of the little Hutchisons sat in the corner of the kitchen, rubbing their eyes and complaining.

"You can take the children home. I'll watch this."

"Oh, I couldn't—" Mrs. Hutchison cast a glance around the kitchen.

"It's getting late for little ones. I'll manage just fine, I promise."

The woman's face softened in relief. "Thank you, Hattie."

Not long after Mrs. Hutchison and the children had headed out into the wintry night, Isurus appeared in the kitchen. "Do you want help?"

Mrs. Goff sniffed pointedly from over by the pies.

Hattie went to the stove and began stirring the soup to keep it from sticking. "I'm fine. I don't want you making those hands worse."

Isurus settled on a stool near the stove. "Quite the storm out there. As bad as the night I washed up."

"How did you happen to—wash up? Without any wreckage?"

He shrugged. "Don't take rides from sailors when you have a glowing tattoo. Apparently, you look like bad luck when a storm's brewing."

Hattie smothered a laugh.

"Miss Scrow…." His voice turned serious. "What is it you want in life?"

She looked up from the soup, surprised. "Well, I guess most girls would tell you they want someone to love them."

"I am not asking about most girls. I want to know about you."

Hattie made slow circles in the broth with the wooden spoon. "I want to do right. I don't have any expectations of changing the whole world, but I want to do well what I've been given to do and make a difference to the people I love."

She tasted the broth, set the spoon aside, and wiped her hands briskly on her apron. "Now you must tell me what you want in life."

Isurus stiffened slightly.

"Come on," she urged, leaning her hands on the long table. "Out with it, it's only fair."

"That's not my choice, really."

"You're a great man where you come from, or so I've been led to believe. I know you must have expectations."

He cleared his throat and began haltingly, lowering his voice out of range of Mrs. Goff's sharp ears. "I want to live with honor, so that when I die, it may be said that I lived well. I want to do what would have made my father proud."

Hattie studied his earnest face for a long moment. "That wasn't so bad," she said softly.

She took up a rag to protect her hands and lifted the pot from the stove. "I'll take that." Isurus stood quickly and reached out to take it.

"You should go on home, Isurus. It's late."

Gently he took the pot from her hands. "No, I am staying to walk you home. It is nearly midnight, and the weather is not improving."

"Well, I'm staying until Winters comes in and his men have had something warm in them, however long that is."

"Then I will wait. I am in no hurry."

Isurus walked Hattie home in the pale, wild morning, just after dawn. Winters's boat never came in.

Hattie stood on the rocky edge of the wooded heights and gazed out, letting the wind wash over her. The sky was gray and fretful, blowing a fine spray of rain and sea-mist up into the air. From this wild vantage point, she could look up and down the coast in both directions.

The sea—the beautiful, terrible sea—was dark and choppy, biting at the rocks that held it back from the land.

The town had been full of tears and regrets this morning. She expected no less, for Jack was well loved. But this was life—here in Roke Point, it was only a matter of when and whom.

And this time, it had been Jack.

The loneliness was keenest now that the funeral was over and there was nothing but to go home, missing him, feeling keenly the empty place that would never be filled. She couldn't imagine what it was like for Lettie, alone with the twins.

The wind caught at the skirt of her black dress, pulling her gently, like a dog asking to go on a romp. But she was as dull and unfeeling as the moss-covered rocks beneath her feet. Everything, from the sighing pines to the angry sea to the seabird suspended on the easterly wind, seemed to be mourning today.

It was all a perpetual gray, blurring slowly.

"Miss Scrow!"

Hattie glanced up, wiping her tears away swiftly.

Isurus stood at the head of the trail leading back to town, his hands thrust into the wide pockets of his coat.

"I did not mean to disturb you. I thought—I didn't think anyone was up here."

"No, please…stay." She dug in her pocket for her handkerchief and blew her nose. "I just couldn't stand to go home just yet. Jack hasn't even lived there for two years, but the house is…it's full of memories."

"Naturally."

"I just—I just really thought they would make it. Something must have gone wrong. Mr. Winters and Jack, the other two hands…they knew the sea."

"The sea takes, without cause or care. Even the best of her children die by her hand."

"Is it strange, then, that I take refuge in being near it?"

"No." Isurus shook his head and crossed the needle-carpeted ground between them. "To your people—and to mine—the sea is everything."

Hattie gave a sad smile and lifted her face to the spray. "I think I was made for the sea, and the sea for me. Perhaps it's strange to love such a terrible and bloodthirsty thing; I don't know. In this town we pit ourselves against it, day after day, for our whole lives, knowing every day that this could be the day the sea wins. Yet I am not afraid of it. I love it, even." Hattie's voice was quiet against the insistent wind.

"I think that is something we sea-folk must live with."

"Like being torn in half."

For a space, it was only the wind.

Hattie swallowed. "I wanted to thank you. For the vanilla. I keep thinking of what I said about waiting for a special day, and it—it seems silly, but I put it in the cookies I made him for his birthday, and I had no idea that it was—his last—"

She took a deep breath and couldn't go on.

Gently, like a whisper, she felt his warm hand on her shoulder. The words came pouring out again. "He left behind Lettie, who adored him, and the twins—he loved them, and they won't even remember him. And Mr. Winters, he always had candy in his pockets for the children—he loved children, even though he never had any of his own—it all seems so wrong. I just—I just want to see Jack again. I want to know what happened, I want this all to come undone, and I don't want to go on. Not without them."

Isurus cleared his throat, and his words came slowly, as if each carried a weight that he was hesitant to lay on her.

"Life is a flame—bright and suddenly gone. There is no oracle written among mortals which declares to each their days. Sometimes our hope is like a curse, showing us things we wanted but which were not to be. But be assured that Jack's death was not meaningless. A full life is not measured in years."

Hattie nodded, turning away to wipe a tear with her fingers.

"Thank you. I hadn't thought about it that way before."

"Neither had I, until I was faced with the prospect of my own death." He looked at her solemnly. "My father was king of Atlantis, and upon his death this spring, I was crowned in his place. Three months later, I was passed the death sentence myself."

Hattie wiped her face again and looked up at him in astonishment, wondering how he had carried such a secret alone for so long.

"All my life, I had been prepared and educated for one purpose. A purpose which, after mere months, I failed."

Her throat was dry. "And?"

"I had to take comfort from the knowledge that I had done no wrong. Who are we to say what must be? Perhaps the life that seemed wasted to me would bring about some good, whether or not I lived to see it."

Hattie swallowed, blinking into the cool wind. Her voice sounded small to her ears. "You were the king."

He thrust his hands into his pockets and nodded.

She let out a shaky sigh. "I am surprised you could be so…calm. After losing so much."

He looked at her with understanding. "We have words we recite in memory, in Atlantis: 'All sorrows shall pass, pass into the dawn; and in a river of joy, we shall forget our sorrow.'"

"It's beautiful."

"Those words were fresh to my mind, from my father's passing. And they comforted me."

Isurus stood like a carven statue, looking east, toward the blurred horizon. The wind played with his hair, and he swallowed. Hattie could see the movement of his throat, the longing in every taut muscle of his body. His eyes were gray-blue like a sorrowful sea.

It was as if a memory had taken him and he was, for the moment, no longer in Maine.

"Do you miss it? Atlantis?"

He glanced back at her, and the faraway look was gone.

"I miss the Atlantis that could have been." His voice was quiet, but not sad. "The one I thought I would have."

Hattie felt suddenly almost too tired to stand. The wind cut through her like a knife, and she shivered.

Quietly, Isurus took off his coat and tucked it over her shoulders. The arm he offered her glowed a faint blue beneath his good shirt.

"Take courage," he whispered. "All sorrows pass."

Once, he had asked her why she loved the old texts so much.

Beauty, she had said.

"But most of them are full of doom," he had replied.

"Yes." Her eyes had lit when he said that. "That is what makes the good prophecies so beautiful. A single candle can be seen across the water in the dark, while a great fire can hardly be seen in the full sun. The texts of doom are there to help us see what we are truly meant to see."

But he had not understood her then.

SIX

And So Farewell

"Now, you must be good to him when he comes. No teasing," Hattie warned Fred as she took his coat and scarf.

"What, can't he handle it? No man can be interested in my sister and not take teasing."

"Shh." Hattie held up her hand. "We have invited him for Christmas because he will be leaving soon. It's more of a…farewell."

Fred lowered his voice. "And you?"

Hattie shook her head. A knot of regret pinched her stomach. "There's no understanding. Don't embarrass me, Fred, please."

"I will not tease him—much." Fred's voice was solemn, but his eyes danced.

"I'll hold you to it."

The door opened and Isurus slipped in almost silently, so unlike the hearty greetings they had received from her brothers.

"Come in, my friend!" called Fred, who had already bounded away to begin lighting the candles on the tree. "Merry Christmas!"

Isurus shrugged off his coat and handed it over, then unwrapped his snow-crusted scarf. "Merry Christmas, Hattie," he said quietly, as if he had practiced it and wanted to get the words out before he forgot them.

"Merry Christmas, Isurus." She forced herself to meet his eyes bravely. "Please—make yourself at home."

That evening, as the coffee and spiced cider were being poured, Letitia went over to the piano.

It had been a strange Christmas without Jack, but all day they had put a brave face on things, trying to laugh even when the hole he left was as big as a boulder. "Let's finish the night with a few songs," Lettie said. "It wouldn't be Christmas without it."

"I fear I know few of your songs," said Isurus softly, stepping near to Hattie.

"You'll get the idea." Fred elbowed him good-naturedly. "Just pretend until you get the words. The choruses are usually easy."

Hattie could hear the slow, hesitant rumble of Isurus's voice beside her as he tried to keep up with "The First Noel" and "Auld Lang Syne." Her heart swelled at it.

She felt so right, so whole with him beside her. She couldn't say at what moment or time he had come to mean so much to her. But he was, and she was glad of it tonight.

One of the twins began to cry across the room in Chris's arms, and Lettie pulled back from the piano with a sigh. "I really should get them home. But let's sing one more, yes? We always used to end with 'O Holy Night.'"

Her fingers moved gently across the keys, and Hattie's father led the way with his deep voice.

Hattie closed her eyes as she sang, savoring the smells of coffee and spiced cider, the warm sweetness of the baked ham, the sound of singing—her favorite voices all around her.

A thrill of hope! The weary world rejoices, for yonder breaks a new and glorious morn....

For a moment she could pretend, pretend that they were all whole and together, forget that Jack was gone and Isurus was leaving, feel one more fleeting time that all was right with the world.

Lettie played one last lingering time through the chorus, as if she felt the same way; and then it was done.

Hattie opened her eyes as the song finished. Life was moving on around her, relentless as ever, but the feeling of that moment—she would have it to hold against all dark and sorrowful times.

Fred and Margaret took Lettie and the twins home, beginning the good-nights for all.

Hattie's father slapped Chris on the back and shook hands all round before retreating to the sitting room to smoke his pipe, leaving Hattie to see Isurus out the door.

He was winding his scarf around his neck slowly, as if he too were holding on to this night as long as possible, when he looked hesitantly at Hattie.

"Could we go for a stroll before I say goodnight?"

"Of course." She felt a keen pang of sorrow. "I will get my coat."

The night was lit by the moon reflecting off the fresh snow, and the air was clean and cold. Beyond the house, the sea washed mildly against the shore.

For a few minutes, they walked in silence.

"Somewhere," Isurus said at last, with an effort, "somewhere across that horizon is home. Perhaps they are singing for me 'Farewell, and farewell,' and here I am, like one struck dumb, unable to answer their call."

Hattie cast about for an answer but could find nothing to say.

"I want to go to them," he whispered.

"But you are." It seemed strange that he should be talking like this, now that he was so close to leaving.

Isurus nodded, and she felt the ache in him. "As king, your life is bound up with the kingdom. I am separated, but I feel the strain in every nerve. When I am not in Atlantis, I am in pain."

Hattie nodded, swallowing past the lump in her throat.

"I want you to know—Hattie—that you have been a comfort. When I am with you, the pain of being away lessens."

"You mean it, Isurus?"

"Yes. And—" He cleared his throat. "I cannot ask you to marry me. To put on you that burden, the sudden strain of expectation and danger, it would not be fair. But—but I know that we are fond of each other, and under different circumstances—"

Hattie kept her eyes facing out toward the icy sea. "Will your brother fight you for the throne?"

"To be sure."

"How far is Atlantis?"

"Across the sea. Nearly as far as Greece."

"Ah."

He reached out and took her hand. "So you see, that is why I cannot ask you—why it would be unfair."

"To ask me to leave my home and live in yours? Isn't that what being married is?"

"It isn't like moving down the street. You said once you expected to live and die here."

"Well, I did, because I didn't expect to love you." Her throat tightened as the words left her mouth.

"No woman of Atlantis would agree to leave it just for a husband."

"Well, thank goodness you found a solid Maine girl, then. We're really not scared of much."

There was a sudden silence. Even the sea seemed to hold its breath.

"You mean you would say yes, if I asked you?"

"I would."

Isurus bit his lip. "No—no, I cannot. I will not. It is not fair to you, whatever you say."

"Why not, Isurus?"

"Because there could be danger. And the situation may be…ugly." His grip on her hand tightened. "Have you ever seen a caged animal bloody and kill itself against the bars, trying to be free?"

Hattie nodded.

"Being king and unable to rule is like that. I must try for that kingship until I regain it or die."

She twined her fingers in his. "That's why I don't want you to be alone."

Isurus turned his face away, but he did not pull his hand from hers. The sound of the sea filled the space between them.

Her heart was beating faster than before. "Isurus, ask me. I won't regret it."

She heard him take in a long breath.

"Isurus, please."

She heard him swallow.

"Harriet Scrow, will you be my wife?" he said softly.

"Yes," she whispered. "I will."

Tears stood in his eyes when he turned back to her, but he laughed. "I thought I was going to say goodbye, not ask to marry you."

"I did too." Laughter sprang from her throat to meet his.

He lifted her hand to his lips and kissed it. "Thank you, Hattie."

"I wouldn't wish anything else."

He released her hand and they started back slowly toward the house.

"You aren't at all what I imagined marrying," Hattie smiled, swinging her arms and clasping them behind her back.

"Oh." He looked crestfallen and opened his mouth to speak, but nothing came.

"I don't care." Hattie looked up at his sad face and laughed. "I don't care at all, if it means I can be with you."

"You mean it?"

"I wouldn't say it if I didn't."

He shook his head with a smile. "What are we going to tell your father?"

"He will understand. He likes you anyway, so that will make it easier."

He stopped before the door, looking down at her with a gentle, happy light in his eyes. "I will wait a while for the wedding, if you like."

Her heart gave a twinge. She had seen the pain in his face as he looked across the water. "Can you?"

He gave a single nod.

"Spring, then." She reached for his hand and squeezed it with a laugh. "I always thought spring would be a lovely time for a wedding."

SEVEN

Sweet to Salt

When Hattie's mother died, she told her daughter two things: Be strong for your father, and be good.

Hattie had tried to do both.

She studied herself carefully in the mirror, from her chestnut hair, pinned up in an elaborate bun, to the pure white dress that covered her arms and throat in delicate lace. The sun streamed in the windows, a pale April light that left gentle patterns on the wood floor, boards she had scrubbed just yesterday. Boards her mother had scrubbed before her, and her grandmother before that.

Funny, that she should think of that now, on her wedding day.

"Hattie, you look beautiful." Margaret came in and laid the bouquet down on the table.

Hattie turned away from the mirror and crossed the room to take her sister-in-law's hands.

"Thank you."

"I cannot even say how happy I am for you. It is good to see you smile." Margaret put her arms around her in a close hug.

Hattie's heart swelled, whether with joy or sadness she could not say. "It feels good to smile again." She straightened and glanced again in the mirror, taking a deep breath.

"Are you ready?"

"Yes." Hattie smoothed down the skirt of her dress. "I am."

The ceremony was simple and traditional. There was certainly nothing about it to suggest that Hattie Scrow had married the king of Atlantis, except for the bronze ring with the blue stone he slipped onto her finger with his vows.

If the rest of Roke Point had known, the town would have been in a tither for the next three years.

Fred led the toasts in the church hall with all his old wit and humor, and Isurus, from whom the town had barely seen a smile during all his time in Roke Point, laughed thrice. His time at Sackett's had vastly helped his reputation, and he was toasted with no sign of ill will from anyone, not even Mrs. Goff.

He was accepting the well-wishes of Mr. and Mrs. Sackett when Hattie came up beside him and whispered in his ear.

"Dearest, there is a photographer. Father has paid for him to take a wedding photograph, his gift to us."

Surprise and amusement appeared on his face. "We do not need a wedding photograph."

"Just one. Think, when our children are grown, it will be something to show them—the day we were married."

He furrowed his brow. "Will that make you happy?"

She smiled at his earnestness. "Yes, it will."

"Very well." He adjusted his sleeves and collar as if they were too tight. "For them, and for you."

He took Hattie's outstretched hand and followed her to the wall where a chair and a decorative plant stood. "Do you want to sit?"

Hattie shook her head. He picked up the chair and carried it out of the way.

"Thank you, dear," she whispered.

"It is nothing."

Isurus cleared his throat and looked at the camera with a solemn face. Hattie leaned her head against his arm and smiled.

A flash, and it was done.

Late in the afternoon, after all the guests had made their way home full of punch and cake, Isurus drove Hattie down to their new home—a cottage, rented from Sackett, as they were only staying for a month. Isurus had booked steamer tickets for the end of May.

"Well, Mrs. Lamnidae, welcome home." Isurus stopped the horse and trap, borrowed from Chris, and jumped out. He handed Hattie down and led her to the door, unlocking it and lifting her over the threshold in strong arms like a man born and bred in Maine.

After changing into ordinary clothing and setting her wedding flowers in fresh water, Hattie sat down in a kitchen chair and admired the ring Isurus had given her.

It was ancient and brassy and mysterious—not the sort of wedding ring she had ever imagined for herself. The blue stone was dull in the dim lamplight, but at midday, it had flashed like sun on a clear sea.

Isurus emerged from the bedroom, buttoning up a blue flannel shirt. "Hattie, are you tired?"

"No." She smiled broadly. "Not at all."

"Good. Will you come with me?"

"Of course."

Isurus went over and opened her hope chest, pulling out a couple blankets. "Here. We will need these."

He handed them over to her and went to the front hall.

"Are we going out? It's cold tonight!"

"You said you were not tired." He struck a match and a warm glow grew, casting his shadow against the pantry door.

"I am not." She hugged the blankets contentedly. "But—being tired and being cold are not the same thing."

He set the lantern on the table and took his coat down from the peg on the wall. "Here, wear this."

"You will be cold without it! I see it in you already."

He laughed even as he shivered. "No matter, I shall go put on a few more shirts."

Hattie stuck her arms in his warm coat and settled her face into the collar. It smelled like him—salt spray and musty rope and windblown hair—and that was even more comforting than the warmth.

Isurus came out of the bedroom, tugging at the sleeve of one of his shirts. She could see from the collars that he had indeed layered three on top of the original.

"There, it is well now." He grinned sheepishly.

He took up a glass canning jar and pumped fresh water into it until it brimmed.

"Are you ready?"

Hattie stuck her hands into the generous pockets of the coat and nodded.

She followed him out onto the quiet, cold beach. The dry sand shifted and slid under her booted feet, and she leaned heavier on her husband's arm. The early stars had come out already.

"All right?" He looked down at her.

"Yes, quite." She pushed her head against his shoulder. "I'm happy."

"I have never been happier in my life." He leaned down and kissed her, and she laughed, moving closer to him as the wind picked up.

He stopped near a large piece of driftwood. "Here is good enough."

He laid the extra blanket down on the sand and set the lantern beside it.

"What are we doing?" Hattie thrust the hair out of her face and eyed the sea lapping at the soft shore.

"You will see." He gave a little smile. "Come this way."

He led her down to the wet edge of the sea, just where the water turned when the waves rushed ashore. "Stand here."

With the toe of his boot, he traced a large circle around them. The water pulled at it, filling the line, blurring the edges.

He fished in his pockets and dug out a small packet of dark paint powder. "It is not the same, but it will do well enough."

He dipped his fingers in the sea, then ran his thumb down the dry, packed powder. Gently, he drew vertical lines on her forehead and chin.

"Now you do the same."

She dipped her hand in the sea and put her thumb in the paint.

"Across my face. Here—" He guided her thumb across his cheekbones and over the bridge of his nose.

"Is this an Atlantean tradition?"

"Yes. Now you can clean your fingers." He bent down, rinsed his own in the sea, and began to undo his bootlaces.

"Are we taking our shoes off?"

"Yes. Go ahead when you are ready."

Hattie scrubbed her fingers clean with sand and seawater, then unhooked the laces on her boots.

"I will take those." Isurus gathered their shoes up and carried them up to the dry ground. "If you become too cold, tell me."

"Don't tell me we're going swimming," joked Hattie.

"No, but we will walk into the surf." He picked up the jar of fresh water in one hand and held the other out to her. He glanced down apologetically at the hem of her skirt. "Your dress will be wet."

She took his hand with a grin. "Seawater practically flows in my veins. I'll be fine."

He led her out into the surf until the water was halfway between their ankles and their knees. "Now, we take a drink, you and I."

He held the jar as she took a sip, and she held it for him. Then he took it in both hands and poured it slowly into the sea.

"Sweet to salt, flesh to flesh; the stars marry above in constellation against the ebb and flow of time. May the sun shine upon your household, the wind bend your sails toward home, the battle be swift, the welcome fair."

He handed her the empty jar and reached into his pocket, drawing out a box of matches. He struck one and held it between them, the light playing on his sharp nose and the shifting sea-blue of his eyes. He took her free hand in his and held it above the match.

"Now you repeat the first part," he whispered.

"Sweet—"

"To salt," he prompted.

"Flesh to flesh. The—"

"The stars marry above in constellation against the ebb and flow of time." He leaned his forehead against hers.

"The stars marry above in constellation against the ebb and flow of time."

"So be it." He dropped the match into the water, and it snuffed.

"There." He put his long arm around her shoulders. "We are married according to the traditions of Maine and of Atlantis. I may now take you as my queen as well as my wife."

Hattie laughed, cradling the jar against her chest. It was a solemn moment, but she could not help it. Her heart was bursting.

"Are you cold?"

"Only a little."

"Come, I will get you out of the sea." He reached down and scooped her up into his arms, baggy coat and all.

"Enough, I can walk!" she protested, but there was no real objection in her tone. It was strange and wonderful to be loved like this, to let him care for her as though she could break, though her whole life long she had been strong, and proud of it. It was strange and wonderful to be close to him.

He settled her on the driftwood with her feet on the blanket and dried them off before the sand could coat them.

"Now we won't grace the new house with too much sand," he smiled.

"I wouldn't care if we did. My mother used to say sand on the floor was good luck, because it meant your husband had a livelihood."

"Your people put great stock in the ability to work hard."

"Hard work is a good thing, Isurus."

"Yes." He grinned sheepishly and rubbed the back of his head. "But I must get used to you wanting to work your fingers to the bone all the time."

"You will be glad of it when you've worn clean through your socks and need them darned."

"I do not doubt it." Isurus sat and pulled on his socks and boots. He shook out the extra blanket and wrapped it around their shoulders. She leaned against him, feeling the warmth of his shoulder and his arm around her.

"Out here you can see all the stars." He pointed to the

constellations above them, going through the Atlantean names one by one. "There is the Shark, the Boned Fish, the Dog that Ate the Bird…."

Hattie laughed softly. "What odd names you have for the stars. I thought your people would name them after all sorts of ancient legends."

"We do that as well," he chuckled. "We have Pegasus, Achilles—Odysseus's ship."

"Which one is that?"

"See the line of stars there?" He pointed to a belt of three.

"Yes…."

"Directly above, the curved line and the bright star. There it is."

"I like that. Odysseus's ship."

He dropped his gaze from the stars to look her in the face. "My father taught me all these. Many things I had to learn from tutors and warriors and kinsmen, but the study of the stars he reserved for himself. He told me the stars are a man's truest companion, for they make both him and his troubles small in a moment. I have found it to be so."

Hattie leaned her head against his shoulder and tilted her face to the sky. "Tell me more of your names for them."

He slid his arm around her and pointed northward with his free hand.

"Do you see there, beyond the stand of pines? How those stars rise like a peak? That is the mount of the First Atlantean."

"Who is the First Atlantean?"

"He is the founder of our race. And his story is one of our oldest legends. I will tell it to you sometime."

"We have all night," Hattie whispered, leaning in closer.

"Well." He shifted to let her rest her face against his shoulder. "In ancient days, the people of Atlantis were the greatest of the peoples of the world, and their fierceness and power were known to all."

His voice took on the tone of a storyteller, as if he was recalling some old tutor from his youth.

"But they grew proud. So much so that they shook their fists at heaven and did whatever they wished. And the highest of the gods was so grieved by this that he declared a great doom upon our people. The Atlanteans were angered, of course, and troubled in mind, and they fought the judgment that had been handed down from heaven. And so the god relented, and he said that if a sacrifice was made to show that they had changed in heart, the doom would not come upon them.

"But the people were not changed in heart. They remained proud, all but one man—Nalak. He was a good man, faithful in all his deeds, and he pleased the gods well. And the Atlanteans schemed to send him as a sacrifice, a false show of their change of heart. Nalak knew that their repentance was but a show, and it grieved him deeply. But he loved his home and he loved the gods, so he agreed to go to Aralith, the high mountain, as the sacrifice. He went alone, dressed in pure white, according to the words of the highest god; but when he reached the mountaintop, there was no altar, no cave to go within, no place to die, but rather a boat. And even as he looked down the way he had come, the heavens split, though it was not the season for rain, and water poured down, and violent storms took hold of the earth and moved it, and before his eyes, the proud and mighty Atlantis disappeared.

"He lived in his boat for the length of time a shark carries her young—for the waters rose to reach the mountain—and birds fed him, and he befriended the shark kind, who thrive in the water. And at the end of the allotted time, the boat settled upon an island, and there he found a fair woman, a gift from the gods, and they and their sons and daughters built Atlantis as it stands now. And in all our veins runs their pure blood."

Hattie did not realize she was holding her breath until she let it out in a sigh. "Quite a story."

"Whether the details are true or have changed with many years' telling, we honor him in our feasts, remembering how our ancestors paid for their pride—and how the sacrifice of one man was the salvation of our people."

"Mm." Hattie closed her eyes, savoring being close, just them and the sea. Isurus tucked the blanket closer around her and kissed her head gently.

The spring air was cold but full of life; Isurus's arm was around her shoulders, warm and reassuring; and the sea called to them in a rush and murmur.

It was a beautiful night.

PART TWO

Atlantis

The Shark King has come for his own

"Why are you sad?"

He looked up from his book and banished the frown that had marked his face a moment before. Indeed, she was gracious—it was more anger than sadness on his face. "It is raining," he said.

He hated rain. It stopped the hunting and the fishing. His father said it made the flowers and crops and good things grow, but that was little consolation to him. Rain flooded the courtyards, made the horses shy, and was a good excuse for his tutor to make him work at his books.

The only thing that comforted him in this was that she was always with the books, and so they could talk.

"But it will rain at the end of the world," she said.

She was always saying strange things like that.

"How do you know?"

"Because it says 'and world's ending, with sweet to salt, will end.'"

"You think that is rain? I thought it was a wedding."

"It is rain." She sounded sure.

"You are always sure about things."

"So are you—you could be king, the way you carry yourself."

"But I was not born to be a king," he had said. "It is not my fate."

"Fates may be many things," she said. "No man may know or understand his fate—not completely. We are bound to them. But if one is bound to a thing, the thing is bound to him. We spin our destinies as much as they spin us."

He had thought about this and abandoned it; it whirled around too swiftly, like a child's toy.

"Well, I wish I could be king," he had admitted.

EIGHT

The Shark King Returns

The warm Mediterranean wind gusted over the deck of the steamer, whisking Hattie's hair back. The sea was a blinding blue, and in the far distance, nestled in the heart of the deepest blue, rose a low chain of islands, strung out like pearls upon a fine lady's necklace.

Isurus's hand found hers on the rail. "Here—" he gestured to the rolling expanse— "is the land of my fathers."

"Those islands?"

"Those are just the outer ring, mainly uninhabited. Atlantis is hidden beyond." His face melted into a swift, bright smile. "But I often ventured far into these waters as a boy."

Hattie leaned into Isurus and laughed, letting the wind carry the sound of it away over the wide water.

His arm stole around her shoulders. "At long last, we are here."

"And what will they say when they see you again?"

Isurus looked soberly toward the horizon, all laughter gone from his voice. "My survival proves my innocence."

"So you have said." A quiet uneasiness crept into Hattie's heart. She wound her fingers more tightly into his. "But I can't help having a bad feeling."

Isurus planted a kiss in her hair. "Don't worry, my love."

Her uneasiness did not die, but she shoved it away, looking down into the water. A school of fish darted about just beyond the wake of the ship, parting around the lazy gray form of a hammerhead shark.

"Look." She pointed down as its fin broke the water.

"He's large." Isurus made a noise of approval in his throat. "A

Sphyrna, like my friend Mokarran."

"A shark?"

"A *Sphyrna*. A hammerhead, as you say. It is his kind."

"Your friend is a shark?" Hattie pressed. She had heard Isurus speak of Mokarran many times, but this was something new.

Isurus laughed. "No, no—he's a man. But the sharks are as our brothers, and he is of a kind with the hammerhead."

"I see." It was going to take some getting used to, this strange world of people all befuddled and mixed in with sharks.

"A fine sight, isn't it?" A deep voice sounded over her shoulder. Her heart gave a little jolt. The ship's captain, a tall, bearded man, had come up behind them and was peering at the horizon.

"To be sure." Isurus leaned back a little to face the man, answering with cool ease.

"Ever been to Athens before?"

"No. Neither of us."

"Well, you'll be there by tomorrow morning." The captain rubbed his long nose and gave them a wink. "You'll enjoy it." He moved down the deck, greeting other passengers who had come up for air.

Isurus put his head down near Hattie's, his voice wry. "'Tis a pity we shall not get to enjoy Athens."

Early moonlight slanted over the deck, leaving one side drenched in deep shadow. Hattie had slept only an hour or two before Isurus woke her, and they had worked as silently as possible, gathering their baggage in the dark.

When she asked about the watch, he merely said that it had been seen to; and it was true. Not another living being stirred on the deck.

Now they waited.

The moon, glinting off the sea, threw soft light up into Isurus's lean face. He gazed down into the dark water as if he could pierce its depths.

The line of his shoulders told Hattie he was tense.

"Who is coming for us?" she murmured.

"I don't know. Perhaps my friend Mokarran, perhaps another he sends. There—" He withdrew swiftly from the side, bending down to shoulder the baggage. "They are coming."

A dark vessel was materializing out of the blackness, startlingly close, cutting the already fractured moonbeams with its wake. It seemed to be a flat-decked boat, no larger than her kitchen at home. Its prow and sides were hung with dark cloth—it seemed either to be in mourning or in disguise, concealing the gilt that winked from underneath as the wind stirred the cloth.

Isurus put his face near hers so he could speak softly. "A man will come up for the trunk. Are you ready?"

Hattie nodded.

It was a long way down, but the sea was calm and the ladder swayed only gently beneath their weight. Hattie seemed to climb forever before she heard Isurus drop to the deck of the ship below them and his voice, a little breathless, came up to her: "Easy, just a small jump."

Hattie let go of the ladder and dropped.

Her boots hit the smooth wood with a dull thump; Isurus's hand was immediately offered to steady her.

She took it, then glanced up swiftly, for the touch of his hand felt different.

A hum had begun the moment Isurus set foot on the deck—whispered orders, words she did not understand—but he stood as if heedless of it all. His fingers, touching her hand, were all grace; his back straight as a mast, but not stiff; his eyes were as distant as the stars.

Her quiet, understated husband was no longer at her side. This was a king, waiting for his crown.

A single figure stood across the deck from them. A glance over her shoulder showed three men bowed with their foreheads to the deck, and beyond them, the lights of the steamer pulling away.

For a single moment, tears rose in Hattie's throat as the last shred of her old life faded into the night.

The dark figure standing across from them broke his silence. "Let Atlantis take back her own, forgiveness ask of the sea for a task it was not to bear."

The man came forward—he wore a long white tunic and a collar of twisted, jewel-studded metal that encased his shoulders and throat—and pressed his forehead against Isurus's sturdy boots. "Welcome, Isurus Lamnidae, Shark King, Lord of the Sun Throne, ruler of Atlantis and the surrounding seas."

"Rise, Galeio Triakidae. Long may your house stand."

Galeio rose and withdrew a few steps. He had a lean, pleasant face, carefully void of any expression, gray hair tempered with brown, and bright blue eyes that even the dim light could not hide. They flicked briefly to meet Hattie's gaze. She met them steadily.

His face gave her the same sense of danger that Isurus's had when first she met him, but Galeio's was dangerous because it was smooth and veiled—a man you could watch for hours and never know what he was thinking.

"This is a small welcome for the attrition of an ungrateful people." Isurus's voice was quiet.

"Judge not the people, sovereignty. It was Mokarran's wish to make your return as secret as possible. I come bearing the duties of all."

"Then fulfill them. But first—greet my queen."

A brief glint of understanding came into Galeio's eye, and he looked at Hattie again as though seeing her for the first time.

He pressed his palms together, and his single earring, a cluster of gold, swung as he bowed his head. "Sweet to salt, flesh to flesh; the stars marry above in constellation against the ebb and flow of time. Welcome, my queen. My life and my duty are yours until the stars fall and the seas overtake the world."

He looked up briefly into her face and smiled. It was a kind smile, almost boyish, but still under that veil of smoothness.

Isurus's voice broke in on them. "You may proceed."

To Hattie's surprise, he was unbuttoning his shirt—the very one Mr. Sackett had given him for Christmas.

The shirt fell to the deck. Heedless of ceremony, Hattie scooped it up and folded it. There was no sense in wasting a good shirt.

One of the bowing men brought Galeio a folded tunic on which was laid a set of armbands and a circlet. Galeio took them solemnly and turned to Isurus. "Let Atlantis bring atonement to the one who has been wronged, paid in gold—" he clasped one band on Isurus's outstretched wrist— "and silver." Isurus held out the other wrist to receive the second band. "And a garment of pure white. Our sins be upon our heads. The sea has judged you clean."

Isurus took the tunic and pulled it over his head. It was white and soft and made from the finest linen Hattie had ever seen. Not even her mother's wedding tablecloth had been of such a fine weave.

"And to our king we give homage. May the light of Atlantis ever grace your brow."

Isurus inclined his head slightly as Galeio set the golden circlet upon his dark hair.

Almost immediately, Isurus straightened, taking off the silver bracelet.

"This is yours, Hattie—the first of the offerings Atlantis shall make you."

Hattie looked up into Isurus's face, and for the slightest moment, the king-light in his eyes warmed. "Go on. It will look far better on you than on me."

He kissed her hand briefly, then fixed his solemn gaze again on Galeio. "Forgiveness is granted, the atonement accepted. As a son, I come home. As the Shark King, I come for my own."

Hattie clasped the band around her forearm. It was cool and heavy, shaped like twisted olive branches and studded with green jewels for the leaves.

She wondered if the opulence was because they had nearly killed him or because he was king.

A couple voices broke out across the deck and Galeio's head turned suddenly, reminding Hattie of a hawk. "Keep quiet," he ordered.

"The gates," Isurus murmured, leaning close. "We are nearly there."

The boat edged into the shallows, the hull grinding slowly against the soft sand.

"This way." Isurus gave Hattie a hand out onto the wet ground.

They were beached on a bare, lifeless spit of sand, surrounded by the sea. Galeio jumped down beside them, and with a shove of strong oars, the boat slid back out into the dark water.

The night was suddenly lonely, just her and Isurus and this man with the smooth manner.

They set out across the spit, the wind raising sand and flinging it at them as if to drive them away. On the far side, at the water's edge, they stopped, and Galeio bent to brush the sand off an ancient-looking set of doors which lay in the ground.

A twinge of wonder and apprehension touched Hattie as she studied the doors, brass-bound and carved with strange, sharp-angled symbols.

They looked heavy, but Galeio hauled them open with ease.

"Sovereignty, welcome home." He glanced up with a pleasant, familiar look, and for the first time, there was no veil in his eyes.

Down a flight of steps waited a single lantern and two horses—beyond, a dark tunnel.

Galeio inclined his head in apology. "We did not realize that his sovereignty had brought a queen. I will walk."

Isurus vaulted onto the back of the nearer horse and reached down to help Hattie up behind him. "We haven't much time, if we wish to arrive by daybreak." He gathered the reins as Hattie settled against his back and wrapped her arms around him. The horse stamped and shifted eagerly below her. "Today, ceremony bows. Take the horse, Galeio. We ride swift tonight."

The morning came upon them slowly and softly. The light around them grew until the tunnel itself changed from black to deep blue, and then to a murky blue-green. When it dawned on Hattie where they were, she nearly gasped.

The tunnels were glass, fathoms below the sea, reinforced with bronze. She had been swimming before in Maine—holding her breath, opening her eyes long enough to marvel at the seaweed and soft sand, the fish flashing like quicksilver—but she had never seen the world beneath the sea so clearly.

She shifted against Isurus's back, drinking in the rocks and the coral, the drifting fish in every color imaginable. A lazy shark cast a thin shadow over them.

"Are you well, Hattie?" Isurus pulled the horse back for a moment, his voice a rumble.

"Just fine."

She leaned her face against his back and let the blue blur as they rushed on again.

Isurus pulled up sharply and Hattie lifted her head, craning her neck around her husband's shoulder. Sunlight had penetrated the sea enough to cast a dancing light upon the travelers. Hattie guessed they were near the surface now, for the water was clear as day.

A pair of horsemen blocked the mouth of the tunnel. Beyond them, the tunnel branched off in half a dozen directions, like the roots of a tree.

One of the men, no older than Isurus, dismounted and strode toward them with a loose, easy gait. He wore a cloak bluer than the sea and a long, high-collared tunic of white, open at the neck. A heavy silver earring dangled from one ear. Yet it was his face that arrested

Hattie immediately: a narrow, fierce face with insolent dark eyes, but one that hid nothing.

He bowed sharply, pressing his fist to his chest.

"I see that my lord Galeio did not fail in what I gave him to do." His voice was deep and rich—not what Hattie expected from one so young and wild-looking.

"It has been fulfilled." Isurus threw his leg over his horse's neck and dropped to the ground. "All is forgiven."

Hattie slid down beside him, her legs a little shaky as her feet touched earth again.

The man glanced once at her, his dark eyes raking her face and outfit with the bold appraisal of a man used to judging character.

His gaze slid slowly from her face to Isurus's. And then he smiled.

The formality Isurus had shown with Galeio was gone. He threw his arm around the young man's shoulder and shook him hard. "Well, Mokarran, you rogue, you have done it!"

The man laughed, his white teeth flashing. "As they say—the king rules, the Shark Kind judge, but Sphyrna makes the waters flow!"

He stepped back, looking Isurus up and down. "And you survived the *idi-kaeth*. Isurus, I cannot tell you how I hoped, how I prayed each day an island would rise beneath you and preserve you. You must tell me the whole tale. I nearly disbelieved when word reached me."

"There will be time for that."

They parted, and Mokarran smoothed his jet-black hair, his eyes going to Hattie.

"This is your wife?"

"Yes." Isurus stepped aside and Mokarran strode to the horse's side. "Hattie, my love, this is Mokarran Sphyrna, the most powerful lord in Atlantis and my truest friend."

Hattie took the long, lean hand the man held out, and he kissed hers with a white, roguish smile. He seemed very young to be the most powerful lord in all Atlantis.

"Sweet to salt," he greeted. "Welcome, Hattie Lamnidae, to the kingdom of Atlantis. Long may the sun shine on you."

"Thank you." Hattie took her hand back.

Mokarran raised an eyebrow at Isurus. "Prionna will be displeased that you have married a foreigner."

"Since when does Prionna have right to dictate a king's choice?"

"Your brother has raised her high, and it is because of her—and because of him—that I meet you today, with Aeris, the Master of War."

Hattie had almost forgotten the second man. He stood beside his horse, watching them stolidly. He appeared older than Mokarran and more strongly built, and he was dressed in flaming scarlet.

"Aeris is Master of War?" Surprise lit in Isurus's face.

"You will find many changes to your kingdom." Mokarran motioned grimly for the other man to come forward.

Aeris walked with the measured stride of a panther. His face was iron hard, but there was a sun-like gleam in his eyes.

"My lord." He bowed with his forehead to Isurus's boots.

"Rise, Aeris, Master of War, and greet my wife." Isurus's familiar fingers twined in Hattie's and drew her forward.

Aeris shook back the folds of his scarlet cloak and held out a hand covered in rings. "To the fair we have been given, we give our fairest." He pulled a ring from his hand—blue and clear like the sea—and placed it on the middle finger of her right hand.

He bowed sharply.

"What has happened that you meet me here, at the crossroads?" Isurus's manner had changed. He was grim again, and Hattie sensed uneasiness in the other men.

Aeris raised his head as if preparing for a fight. "We come to request that you not present yourself to your brother in public."

Instantly Hattie felt Isurus withdraw inside himself. Every door he had opened to her in Roke Point, that he had left open since, slammed.

The muscles of his nearer arm tensed. "And why not?"

Aeris pushed on, his voice like stone. "Altimus rules with a rod of iron. Prionna is deep in his counsel, and she sees all. Suspicion haunts those who were closest to your rule. It goes ill with Atlantis."

His face was calm, but it did not fool Hattie. She had once seen a fight break out between two boat crews on the wharf—they had faced each other thus, braced and defiant.

Nor did it seem to fool the others. Isurus spoke with deadly seriousness. "Then is it not all the more needful that I approach my brother now, even this very hour?"

Mokarran's voice dropped. "Isurus, Crestus is dead."

Hattie heard Isurus's breath stop for a moment. "Crestus, dead?"

"Yesterday in a hunting accident. It was your brother's doing."

Isurus's face went an awful shade of white.

"What cause had he?" His voice shook a little.

Aeris cleared his throat. "None we know of. He raised him to the position of first spear, even as he raised me to Master of War. Crestus was ever a fine hunter."

"And you are sure it was his doing?"

"Without question. There was coin passed to Stellarus, the captain of your brother's guard. An untamed set of hounds was put in for the king's. When Crestus called them back for the kill, they could not be controlled."

"He was betrothed to Zyaena. She is in widow's mourning."

Mokarran's voice was grave.

Isurus put his hand upon Mokarran, drawing his shoulder toward him. "I will honor your sister, and his memory will not die. And yet—" he flung the words at the other men— "with this wicked deed done before you, you wish me not to confront my brother?"

Galeio pressed his hands together. "In hope of your reclamation of the throne…nay, in deep longing for it, we ask this."

"You fear he will kill me?" Humorless laughter rose in Isurus's throat. "You mock me, my friends."

"We do not mock," said Mokarran, his eyes kindling. "If you will not hear me in this, Isurus, I may as well put my knife to your throat and then to mine. His guards now call themselves the Black Tips, and fear of them lies black upon the heart of any who doubt him."

"And what of the Shark Kind?"

Galeio's voice was soft. "They have had worries of their own. Since your brother's ascension, they have remained silent."

"What worries?"

"Portents of doom."

Isurus took in his breath, so soft, so measured, that only Hattie heard it. His gaze went to her face, and for a moment she saw into him. He was torn, torn between deep pain and anger and the need to be brave for his own.

She wanted terribly to reach out and comfort him.

"My heart burns at the thought of his blood lying without answer for even another moment." Isurus's voice was dry, his words measured. "But I will do as you say. I will lodge with you, Mokarran—lead on."

The sun had gone behind the clouds. When Hattie looked up, she saw a great shadow in the water.

NINE

Throes of the Earth

Isurus jerked upright beside Hattie, waking her. The room was dim and close with heat.

"What is it, darling?" she asked, pulling herself up.

Even bleary-eyed, she could see he was covered in sweat. The king's mark on his arm blazed like blue fire in the dim room. A glance at the bright crack in the door seemed to indicate it was close to midday—Mokarran had prepared his finest bedchamber, and they had gone to lie down in the heat of the day, as neither had slept all night.

Isurus ran his hand over his face. "I had a terrible dream," he murmured. "It was like life, but so twisted."

"Would it help to talk?"

He let out a ragged breath. "Perhaps."

"Go on, then." She set a hand on his tense shoulder. "And after you tell me, you can forget it."

Isurus pushed his black hair off his forehead as if it pained him.

"I was in the streets of the city, among the people. I could smell the food from the market, the seawater, the warm air…but everyone was in mourning. And I saw Mokarran walking the streets, crying, 'For shame!' And his fine clothes were in tatters. I stopped and spoke to him, but he could not see me. And then I was a commoner, a fisherman, and I asked Mokarran where the king was."

He took a long, shuddering breath.

Hattie spoke softly. "And did he answer?"

"He said, 'The king is dead—behold the king.' And there, riding on the back of the mighty shark Moraire, the Fate, I saw my brother

Altimus. And Mokarran led me to a thief's pyre, marked with black soot, where a casket was laid. And I was in the casket."

Hattie rubbed his arm, then twined her fingers into his. Her heart tightened at his pain.

"They were burying me at sea, not in the vaults of my fathers. And the people wailed and shouted, 'Where is our king? Why does he abandon us? Why does he not return?' And even as the casket disappeared, I turned, and the palace of my fathers was engulfed in a great pillar of smoke. And Altimus began to laugh, and the—the Lord of the Shark Kind began to say that the time of kings was over, and death reigned, and the palace was to be destroyed."

"Who is the Lord of the Shark Kind?"

"He is the chief of the shark-keepers. He holds more sway in Atlantis than any man—more than I do, even."

"And was that the end of the dream?"

"I thought so." Isurus turned to look at her, his face white. "But as I woke, I heard my father's voice, and he was speaking an old prophecy of doom. And I woke with those words ringing in my ears as if they had been spoken here in this room, right above me."

He looked to her. "The whole dream long, I felt as if I should recognize the events. But not until my father spoke those words did I realize—I was in the prophecy."

"What is it? The prophecy?"

He closed his eyes as though reciting words he had long known by heart. "'Watch, ye sons of the sea, your doom is at hand. With soundless storm rises the fate of Atlantis. With sea's rising and stone's breaking and throes of the earth it comes.' There's more to it, but that's what he quoted."

"Don't worry." Hattie rubbed his shoulder. "You are tired. And you're grieving. It's natural."

"You don't understand." He clenched his fists against the blanket. "According to the dream, I was the doom, not the savior."

"Shh." She pressed her lips to his cheek. "It was just a dream, nothing more."

He let out a long, shaky breath and dropped his legs off the bed.

"I will go to the Shark Kind this very night. I will be named challenger-king. I cannot tarry."

Hattie moved her hand to his back and rubbed again. His muscles were taut. "Just don't be rash," she said gently.

His expression melted a little, and he twisted around and kissed her. "It is not rashness that provokes my decision. Now, I woke you." He patted the warm pillow. "Sleep again, if you can."

The last thing Hattie remembered was the sound of the door closing behind him.

When Hattie saw Isurus again, he was changed. Dressed like an Atlantean in high-collared blue, with sandals on his feet and an earring in one ear, he no longer looked stark and alone, as he had in Roke Point. He was as much a part of this strange world as the bright frescoes on the wall.

The House of Sphyrna was like nothing Hattie had ever seen. It was built of ancient-looking stone, with arches and pillars so ornate that she had nothing in her memory to compare it to, not even from her father's books about faraway places. The room they were in now was courtyard-like, with one side overlooked by stately doors and the other unwalled, open to a quiet expanse of blue water that lapped at the marble steps when the wind blew. A great fountain stood in the center of the room, and the arches that rose around them towered as tall as the lighthouse on Roke Point, rising to an open roof that let in the sunlight.

Little wonder Isurus had never been afraid of heights.

"Did you sleep well?" He came and put his arm around her, and he smelled of strange spices.

"Mhm."

"You are just in time. Come, sit." He settled her beside him on a low couch. "We are about to begin."

"Begin what?"

He smiled. "Taking back the throne."

Hattie noticed a long knife in a black sheath belted on his leg, visible now that he was sitting. Her heart gave a twinge of discomfort, but she said nothing.

Mokarran emerged from another room, bearing a small table with a checkered gameboard etched in its surface. From a box studded with blue and red jewels he produced a number of tiles, each about the size of a large postage stamp, and began to lay them on the board.

Quietly, Isurus reached out and took hold of the table, turning it around. "No, Mokarran," he said quietly. "I will play the usurper."

Mokarran's dark eyes flickered in surprise, but he said nothing. He merely straightened the tiles in their places and placed his hand on the first two on his side.

"Ready."

Isurus gave a silent nod.

They flipped the tiles, revealing markings.

"*Rex* and *carbuncle*." Mokarran's face met Isurus's like a challenge.

"*Trada*," Isurus replied, his face guarded.

Hattie studied the board with a frown. "And this is taking the throne back?"

He never moved his eyes from the board, but he gave a smile of amusement. "After a fashion."

"What is it?"

"It's *ta-para-rex*— 'kill the king.'"

Hattie glanced sideways at him. "That's not a very pleasant name."

He pointed her attention to the game. "There are two sides: the king's side and the usurper's side. He has the tactical advantage, and I must outwit him."

"And how is that done?"

"These tiles represent different powers within the kingdom, but we turn over only a few at a time, allowing our opponent to see some, but not all. To win, you must trick your opponent into a fatal blunder."

A pounding began on the great doors.

Isurus started up, his hand moving to the knife on his leg.

Mokarran rose boldly and waved Isurus away. "I will see to it."

Isurus motioned for Hattie to follow, and they abandoned the game and slipped through the nearest open doorway.

She could feel Isurus's breathing against her arm, hear his steady pulse in her ear as he moved protectively closer to her.

A shadow crossed the floor. Mokarran's voice sounded softly, just around the corner. "It is Taurus. Do you wish to see him?"

After a moment's thought, Isurus nodded, and Mokarran's shadow disappeared.

Isurus turned to Hattie with a wry smile. "You will now meet my cousin, Taurus."

"Is that a problem?"

"No. You—" Isurus's mouth twitched. "You will understand when you meet him."

As they reentered the courtyard, a tall young fellow came bounding in, with Mokarran at his heels.

"Two seas, a usurpation, and the *idi-kaeth!* Nothing keeps you away, my king!"

Isurus had relaxed into as genuine a smile as Hattie had seen him give since their arrival. "Taurus, my cousin, how fare you?"

"Passing well, now that my eyes behold you! I was rot and ruin before." Taurus threw his arms around Isurus in a heedless embrace. "Well, cousin! You look better, not worse, for your exile."

Isurus only smiled quietly.

Taurus released him, flinging the hair out of his face with a toss of his head. He looked like Isurus, except for the lighter brown of his hair, the tinge of green in his eyes, and the crooked scar across the bridge of his nose. His eyes lit on Hattie.

"You must be the queen!" He gave a sharp bow. "I am Taurus Lamnidae."

"Hattie," she replied, holding out her hand.

"Honored." He took her hand and gave it a zealous kiss. "Well, isn't this a strange trick of fate for Altimus? He accuses you of a crime, dethrones you, executes you, and you return looking strong and hale…and with a queen! A very beautiful one, I might add. And it will be on his own head, for he did it all himself."

Hattie flushed, and Isurus reached out and twined a couple of his fingers into hers. "I will be anointed challenger-king tonight. I do not intend to waste time."

"Nor should you! I wish you could knock that pretender off this very hour."

Isurus laughed, but the laugh sounded a little hollow to Hattie.

"Will you take him in combat?" Taurus's eyes danced. "No, fool—what am I saying?"

"No, I want my kingdom, not a public death, but that was a fine thing to say," said Isurus, giving his cousin a shove.

Hattie looked to him for translation.

"My half-brother Altimus," Isurus explained wryly, "once threw twelve stone worth of tiger shark over his shoulder. No one challenges him to combat."

"Alas, 'tis true." Taurus shook his head sorrowfully.

"But of course, I can count upon your loyalty."

"Till the stars fall and the seas overtake the world!" cried Taurus. "After all, I would rather be dead than king of Atlantis."

Isurus shook his head, laughing. "You needn't swear it. I believe you."

Taurus grinned and brushed back his hair with a deft hand.

"I say, Mokarran!" He turned like a fish in the water. "Have you any honey-wine in this place?"

He followed Mokarran into the next room, presumably to find a servant to fetch out food and drink, and Hattie let out a breath she hadn't realized she was holding.

"What does he mean by that? Rather dead than king?"

"Taurus is next in the succession." Isurus's mouth drew upward in a smile. "But he is young and wild. No one wants him on the throne, not even himself. It would be like hitching a colt to a dram. He would break Atlantis, and Atlantis would break him."

"But he can be trusted?"

"Oh, yes." Isurus's eyes took on a gleam. "I have known men like him—merry and frivolous, until you ask them to take up arms for a cause. He is with us. To the worst of deaths."

Hattie thinned her mouth into a hard line. "I wish you wouldn't speak so lightly of death. You didn't in Maine, and now it comes to your mouth so quickly."

"It is a natural part of life."

"Yes, but you all speak of it so frequently and—and easily."

He set an arm around her shoulders. "When there is a crown on your head, there is a knife at your back, Hattie. And men who align themselves with a crown, as these have, invite the same knife. We learn to live with it there."

"Nobody had better try it while I'm in the room," Hattie muttered under her breath.

Isurus gave a short, surprised laugh. "I do believe you mean that."

"You don't grow up with three older brothers and not mean it."

Isurus laughed—a laugh so real it hurt Hattie deep inside—and he put his arms around her. "I love you, Harriet Lamnidae."

He stilled his laughter long enough to kiss her gently.

A throat cleared behind them, and Hattie realized that Mokarran had returned to the *ta-para-rex* board. He lowered his eyes uncomfortably.

"Are we ready to proceed?"

"Yes." Isurus let go of Hattie's hand and strode back to the low couch. "Is it my move?"

Hattie settled in beside him, taking care not to brush the wicked-looking knife in the sheath.

Isurus rubbed his chin with long fingers. "His *rex* is already uncovered."

"That's his king?"

"Yes." Isurus lowered his voice. "But there is one play in the game which can transfer kingship from the *rex* to another piece. If his king is uncovered so soon, he may be planning that move."

Hattie nodded and studied Mokarran. He was bent over the board, his chin in his fingers, mirroring Isurus. His dark eyes gleamed.

"Who is on top?" Taurus reappeared, a tall blue and gold goblet in his hand. He was followed by a servant, who laid out honey-wine and olives and dates on a low table nearby.

"We have hardly begun." Isurus glanced over briefly. "And I see you are exploiting Mokarran's goods. Am I going to find my house in ruins?"

"No." Taurus stretched out on the nearest couch, careful not to spill his drink. "But—perhaps a little different."

Isurus's eyes flicked to his cousin's with a tawny glint.

Taurus rubbed the back of his head uncomfortably. The polished gold of his bracelet caught the sun and scattered it across the walls. "You do not want to see it today, do you?"

"I will not go there today." Isurus reached down and lazily turned over a piece. "If you want a head start."

"I'll take it." Taurus drained the glass and scrambled to his feet. "My queen. My lords—I will see you this evening, or on the morrow."

Isurus and Mokarran rose in a rush and bowed, almost as one, though Isurus's was little more than an inclination of the head.

"Be well," said Isurus.

Taurus was gone like a gust of wind.

"You scared him off," reproved Hattie. "And he was so happy to see you."

"He will not be happy to see me if I find he has used the ancient halls of Lamnidae ill."

Mokarran gave a short laugh.

"What does Taurus do?" Hattie asked. "I suppose he has power of a sort?"

"He has enough power to live just as he pleases. He 'does' very little." Isurus got up and poured himself some watered honey-wine. "But he is keen on *lai-ilith-re*, a very—dangerous sport."

"How is it played?"

He settled himself back beside her on the couch. "The name means 'to steal the prize from the shark.' You must outswim, outsmart, and sometimes wrestle a shark for the prize. A stick with a fish, or a banner dipped in blood. Galeio was once a champion at that game."

Mokarran grunted in agreement. "No one in his age or this was better."

"Galeio?" She would never have guessed it of the smooth-tongued advisor. But thinking back, she recalled a certain restless grace in his movements which reminded her of one of Sackett's men back in Roke Point, a champion swimmer as a young man.

"Taurus tries year after year to get him into the water, but he will not." Mokarran turned over a tile with a quiet clink. "When you left us, Isurus, he swore he would swim no longer."

"Hmm." Isurus took a sip of the honey-wine. "And what did my brother have to say to that?"

"Nothing. He rather depends on Galeio."

"That bodes well for us."

Hattie leaned her head against Isurus's shoulder and gazed up at the open roof. A bank of white clouds was slowly overtaking the square of sky above them.

"*Parida*," said Isurus quietly.

Mokarran gave a low exclamation. Hattie turned her attention to the game as Isurus pulled a tile from Mokarran's side.

"What was that?"

"The traitor. Or—my spy. We have one, each of us, on the other's side. I just pulled a strong piece from him."

"Are you winning now?"

A gleam of fierce mischief lit in Isurus's eyes. He met Mokarran's gaze like a challenge. "I would say my chances are not bad now."

A shadow fell on the room as a cloud passed over the sun.

Mokarran deliberated long on his next move; at last he produced a gold coin and set it upon the table, face up. "Null."

"What does that mean?" whispered Hattie.

Isurus frowned. "Just twice in the game, you are allowed to show nothing and do nothing. The coin is used as a witness to mark the move."

"I see." She looked up from the board.

Odd, it was growing dark.

A tremor rippled below them as if in response to her thought. Isurus started up, seizing her hand in his.

"Quick!" Isurus pushed her under the couch and shielded his head as the *ta-para-rex* pieces rained onto him.

As if from nowhere, a crack of thunder pealed above them. Isurus crouched lower to the ground. His arm, thrown over Hattie's shoulders, tightened fiercely.

Somewhere, a servant screamed. The bottle of honey-wine tipped and smashed, sending shards of glass shooting across the floor.

Then the ground stopped shuddering. As suddenly as the quake had come, it was gone, and the sun shone again.

Mokarran was shouting for the servants already.

"My love, are you all right?" Isurus gave Hattie a hand up and gently dusted her off.

"You're bleeding." Hattie pointed to his ankle, where a red trickle was running down into his sandal.

"Never mind that. It's from the glass. I'll bind it," he said, glancing down at it. "Are you hurt?"

Hattie checked her hands and feet for blood and shook her head.

The floor glittered with glass, mingled with the strewn pieces from the *ta-para-rex* board. Gingerly, she lowered herself onto the couch and began to collect the scattered tiles.

"Dearest, leave be." Isurus gently took the pieces from her hands. "I don't want you cutting yourself."

Her hands shook a little as she wiped them on her skirt. "Is that…normal here?"

Isurus shook his head quietly. He turned to Mokarran. "Has this happened before?"

Mokarran's voice was grim. "Twice, since you left."

A shadow fell over Isurus's face. "It bodes ill."

He strode from the room, trailing blood and glass.

What he hated most was how alike they were. They shared a mother, they shared a tutor, their rooms were alike, the king called them both son.

But because of his real father, his mother's first husband, in the land he did not remember, none of it meant a thing.

A man can have everything and still have nothing.

Without the homage of men, which would pass over his age and strength and fall upon those slim, undeserving shoulders—without the cheers and the looks of adoration, what he had was dust.

No more than dust.

TEN

The Binding of the Fates

The sun was sinking, the daylight growing thin. Mokarran, with a small escort of his personal guard, had seen Hattie and Isurus as far as the hedges that surrounded the shark runs. Now it was just the two of them, walking up the flagstones toward the canals, wide roads of water that reflected the gold and pale pink of the fading sky.

Isurus wore black now, which set off the gold of the collar that encircled his shoulders and neck. Hattie was still trying to get used to the weight of her own collar, similar to her husband's but not quite so heavy.

If only Fred could see her now. He would laugh, and not entirely out of sympathy.

Isurus held her hand tightly. "When we approach the Shark Kind, I will speak. There is but one permissible way to speak to them. But if they look at you, do not be afraid to look them in the eye."

They stepped out of the shelter of the hedges onto a wide, flat strip of pavement that ran along the edge of a deep canal. In the distance stood a small group of men in white.

They were gathered at the water's edge, hooked spears in their hands, their faces grim and impassive. Their tunics were of white and blue, hemmed with gold. Bands of gold bound their arms below the shoulder and at the wrist, and one wore an amber drop in his ear.

The light was dusky, nearly gone now, and the wind blew uneasily at their tunics.

"May the sun ever rise on you and your own," greeted Isurus, putting his hand to his shoulder.

"May the Shark Kind be at peace with you," returned the one with the amber drop in his ear. None of them made a move to step forward and return the gesture.

"How make the runs in my absence?" asked Isurus. "Ever did I come to greet your kind."

The leader inclined his head slightly. His face was narrow, with wistful eyes and a thin mouth. "The Kind are uneasy. There is blood in the water, and they scent it."

Isurus nodded grimly, and Hattie moved a stray hair out of her face. Did they speak of the sharks in the run, or of the state of Atlantis? Or of the portents that Mokarran had mentioned?

"Your brother the king came to see us at the thin moon," said the leader. "He spoke of gold and an everlasting covenant between the Shark King and the Kind."

She could not tell from the man's face if this was a good thing, nor whether by saying it he was threatening or helping Isurus.

"Did he?" Isurus spat.

Her husband's face had nothing soft or tame about it here, beside the shark runs.

Then Isurus laughed, and there was a measured mockery in his tone. "Does he forget that the Shark Kind have no duty to pay the Shark King? I know that as well as any. For this insult of my kin's, I beg forgiveness."

Behind the men, a tall fin cruised about close to the canal's edge, a fin scarred like a fighter.

The leader inclined his head, and Hattie caught a glint of pleasure in his eye that she did not like. "You speak truth with your sharp tongue."

"The truth of a knife's blade is more pleasant to me than kisses from a false mouth."

"May it be so," replied the leader, his tone almost indifferent now. "Why have you come to see us?"

"I wish to be anointed challenger, after the ancient customs. I bring the necessary payment." Isurus drew a cloth-bound package from the breast of his tunic. The tautness of his hands betrayed its weight.

The leader gave a brief nod, and one of the others came forward and took the offered gift.

The man who had taken the gift left them. The rest remained standing out in the wind, saying nothing.

Hattie wished she understood what was happening, but she dared not break the cold silence with a question.

The man returned, and a look passed between him and his leader.

The leader took a step toward Isurus. His glance was a little stonier than before, Hattie thought. "The Lord of the Shark Kind will see you."

He turned and led the group along the water's edge to a majestic building, temple-like, of white and blue stone with a door of a sea-colored gem. He entered in silence, ushering Isurus and Hattie and the others in after him.

Standing just across from the door on a raised step was the Lord of the Shark Kind.

He was not the sort of man Hattie was expecting. His face was smooth, sloping cleanly from angle to angle as if made of marble, and no gray lightened his brown hair. And yet his eyes—mild blue, like the shallows of a tidal pool—were ancient as if he had seen a thousand years.

A strange, haunted feeling crept into her chest. She could not, for the life of her, tell if he was old or young.

"To what purpose do I see you in my halls?" the man asked in a deep, lazy voice, his arms folded. His voice filled the space, though he seemed to be making no effort to raise it. His tunic gleamed a brilliant blue, the light from a hundred candles playing with the blue drops of glass in his ears.

"I have returned, even as Nalak the First Atlantean returned over the sea waves, and have come to take up the mantle of challenger. In nothing do I shirk the blood within me or the mark upon me."

"After committing the *ra-naet-eveg*, you make bold to return?"

"Though death was allotted me, the sea made its judgment, and I return absolved. Atonement was rendered, my forgiveness accepted."

"By the laws, you speak passing well," said the Lord of the Shark Kind without emotion.

Isurus inclined his head in thanks. "One thing more I wish to say."

The Lord of the Shark Kind indicated for him to continue with a brief gesture of two fingers.

"Just this night past, I dreamed of Moraire, the Fate."

The folded arms unfolded, and the man seemed to grow taller. There was an uncertain murmur among the other keepers.

The Lord of the Shark Kind's eyes remained fixed upon Isurus, as if he was dropping a lead within him and fathoming his depths. "What did she in the dream?"

"My brother stood upon her. And then a great doom fell upon Atlantis."

"And you are sure that it was she?"

"It could have been no other. I saw her, you recall, when I was a lad of seven years."

"And it was the last time she was seen. What did you do after this dream?"

"I woke and spoke to my wife. I was uneasy in heart."

The Lord of the Shark Kind's eyes lit for the first time on Hattie, studying her for a moment, intensely. Hattie looked him in the eye and returned the scrutiny.

"You have married a foreign woman."

"Yes."

"Hm." He turned to the man with the amber drop in his ear and spoke a brief word. The man nodded and left, taking the others with him.

"My heart is against your appointment. I see only sorrow and tears for Atlantis."

"It is my right," said Isurus, softly.

Hattie's gaze went to the Lord of the Shark Kind's face, her jaw hardening defensively, but the man did not look at her.

"Two kings have not vied for the throne of Atlantis in many ages. The land is restive, the sharks uneasy. If you take your right, the result will be blood and the coming of doom."

"My brother is already causing blood to come upon the throne and the name of the Shark King. The sea spared and absolved me. I wish to save my land from his rule."

The Lord of the Shark Kind gave a brief bow, and Hattie saw him shutter his thoughts behind impassive eyes.

"Then I will anoint you, after the customs and laws of Atlantis. Come."

He turned and led them further in, into a dim, cool room that smelled of salt and incense. It was bare but for candles and stone carvings on the wall. At the head of the room waited a small, empty platform.

"Remove your cloaks."

Without a word, Isurus unclasped his and handed it over. Hattie followed suit.

"Come, kneel."

The stone was cold and hard as Hattie knelt beside Isurus. The Lord of the Shark Kind stood upon the small platform, washing his hands in a bowl of water. As he dried his hands, a couple drops splashed upon the stone in front of her.

"Is it your wish to become challenger-king and invoke these rights and fates?"

"It is." The flame played on Isurus's marble face.

"Do you understand that by this invocation, you bind yourself to the fate of victory or death?"

"I do."

"Do you wish also to bring to this fate your wedded, as queen?"

Isurus turned to Hattie, his eyes vulnerable in his stony face.

He was afraid. Afraid now to lose her, lose what they had.

In that moment, she resolved she would be his strength, not his weakness. She looked him in the eye and nodded, almost imperceptibly.

"Let her come," Isurus said at last. "But upon my death, let her be freed from this oath."

"So shall it be." Reaching into a carved depression in the wall, the man opened a small, bejeweled casket and removed a flask. Isurus put his hand upon it.

"By the sea, by the stars, by the Shark Kind ever watchful, do you swear your right is just?"

"I swear this."

"And in this path you swear to honor the unbreakable laws or suffer death?"

Isurus's voice was steady—almost too steady, it seemed to Hattie.

"I do swear."

"With this oath, I bind you to this path, until victory or death."

"So be it." Isurus withdrew his hand and bowed his head.

"I therefore anoint you challenger-king, and with you, your queen."

The Lord of the Shark Kind took the flask and poured the liquid upon Isurus's bowed head. It smelled sweet and strong, and somehow—Hattie could not put her finger on quite why—like the sea.

It matted down his dark hair and dripped like blood from his ear to his shoulder. The Lord of the Shark Kind dipped his fingers into Isurus's hair and touched Hattie's forehead with the excess oil. His hand was cool and smelled of salt water and sandalwood.

It took all of Hattie's self-control not to shrink from his touch.

"Rise then, challenger-king." His voice filled the small room the way the sea filled the lighthouse in a storm. "I bid you go in peace."

A lamp burned on the table in the courtyard, bravely pushing against the prevailing dark. Hattie leaned her head against Isurus's shoulder, watching as the stars came out slowly above them.

He reached out and rubbed her hand with his thumb, as if the movement had suddenly reminded him she was there.

"Isurus, are you all right?"

He let out his breath softly.

"I am well. Do not worry on my account."

Hattie pulled her gaze from the stars and reached up to brush his hair back off his forehead. "But I want to know what worries you. My shoulders are strong enough to help."

He shifted, stretching and putting his arm around her. "Much has changed in the year I've been gone. The Lord of the Shark Kind was not glad to see me. If the laws had not given me the right, he would not have anointed me. Of this I am sure."

"What is he afraid of?"

"Who knows? But the word doom is on too many lips, and it worries me that it is on his as well."

"Do you think you did the right thing?"

The vigor returned to his voice. "Of course. Did you see the fear in the eyes of my men, men who have known and loved me from the day I was born? Altimus is a tyrant, wrongfully crowned at the cost of my blood. If I am to save my people, I have no other course but to take back my crown."

Hattie pressed close against him, tightening her grip on his hand. "Well, if you're doing the right thing, it's all right, then."

Isurus smiled sadly. "Galeio thinks the lords will come if I call them, but I am not so sure. I sense that Atlantis is troubled with something worse than my brother."

"Like what?"

Isurus took a deep breath and pushed back the troubled look in his eyes. "I don't know."

"How well do you trust Galeio?"

"Enough to know that he is on my side. He was to my father as Mokarran is to me. Why?"

Hattie shifted uncomfortably. "I don't know. His manner is too smooth. I'm not sure yet what I think of him."

"I've known him my whole life."

She did not want to hurt him, but she had to say it. "And you knew Altimus your entire life."

She felt the change in his breathing, the slight catch in his chest. "I just want you to be careful," she said softly.

"Always, Hattie."

"Must you win the lords? Is it they who will force your brother to abdicate?"

He touched the place on his shoulder where the blue glowed through his garment. "Without force, he will never give up the throne. The vows a king takes are solemn as death, the king's mark unable to be removed. Two men may not bear the mark at once."

"And the lords must decide between you?"

"There is one other way, but it is a last resort."

An uneasiness stirred in Hattie's middle. "And what is it?"

"It is called the *sacitha*, the Test of Kings. They slash a cut—usually on the ankle, or the leg—and you must both swim the runs with the king's hounds."

"The king's hounds?"

"The pack. The hunting sharks. And the one who is not torn apart is the true king."

A sick flash of fear ran through her. Without thinking, she pressed her hand against her mouth. "That's—barbaric."

His arm tightened around her. "Don't give it too much thought, Hattie. I am not doing it, and it hasn't been done in centuries."

"Even so." She tried to thrust the images of blood and fear out of her mind. "The very idea repulses me."

Isurus was quiet for a moment. "As it should," he murmured at last. "I suppose you will find many things about us barbaric. Perhaps even me."

Hattie leaned back against him, letting her heartbeat slow. She swallowed. "Not you."

He kissed her forehead. "I pray so."

"I love you, Isurus. That counts for a lot." Hattie pressed closer, as if by doing so she could convince them both beyond all doubt. "We'll make it."

"I just—I wonder if I have been fair to you, bringing you into such a strange world."

"That's nonsense. My ancestors came over the sea to make a life in Maine. How is that any different?"

"It's just you," he said. "They had each other."

"And I have you. You're as good as any odd assortment of neighbors and cousins, don't you think?"

But he only smiled, a little sadly.

A knock came from the outer doors—soft, secretive.

Isurus rose to his feet in a single swift movement. "Stay here."

"Isurus, no." Hattie started to her feet.

"I will only look," he assured her.

Mokarran came hurrying down the hall to the rescue—blessed Mokarran—dressed in a plain white tunic, no finery to be seen save a heavy gold earring hanging in one ear. "Stay out of sight, I will see to it." He gave Isurus a brief wave to get out of sight and went to the door.

"Should he…send a servant?" asked Hattie, apprehension rising in her stomach.

"In his hands I leave the decisions as to whom should be trusted. At present." Isurus put his arm around her as they drew out of sight behind a pillar.

They heard the door open.

"My lord Mokarran." The voice was familiar, smooth and low. "I bring news that you and his sovereignty will wish to hear."

"He is here." Mokarran's footsteps echoed in the courtyard as he led Galeio in. "Give your news."

Isurus and Hattie stepped from the shadows, and Galeio greeted them with a deep bow.

"What is this news?" Isurus folded his arms.

"This very night, Altimus Carcharodon has visited the Shark Kind to seek their advice. He asked for the fates to be cast, to determine the meaning of today's portent."

Isurus let his breath out in a near-laugh of disbelief, glancing at Hattie. They must have barely missed him.

"And what did he discover?"

"Sovereignty, the lots would not speak. Again and again it was tried, and they gave no answer."

A shadow passed over Isurus's face. "And was a reason found?"

Galeio's bright eyes were hooded and careful. "Altimus became angry and demanded that they cast their own lots, not the king's, to find the reason. So they did as he asked and cast the lots that the Shark Kind use."

It was silent between them for a long-held moment.

"You have come to tell me, you may as well say it," said Isurus softly.

"The lots told Altimus that there was another king in Atlantis. The fates are bound, and they will remain thus, until one of you is dead."

Isurus's voice was low, his calm carefully held. "And what did my brother say to this?"

"It disturbed him deeply. I have never seen him take ill news so quietly, but I fear there will be a great reckoning."

"Does he know of me?"

"No. But he must begin to suspect before long."

"I thank you for bringing me word."

"I would not dream of anything else."

Another thought struck Isurus. "How did the Lord of the Shark Kind take the news? Did he say anything?"

"His face showed nothing. I could have sworn that he muttered 'fool' once, but—" Galeio stopped short, a terrible look crossing his face. "You went tonight?"

"We must have missed my brother by no more than an hour."

"So." The word was little more than a sick gulp.

Isurus looked from Galeio to Mokarran. "Do you have something to say?"

Mokarran opened his mouth with a gentle sound, then shut it.

Isurus spoke with quiet resolve. "You must take your leave, Galeio. You should not be seen here."

"Yes, my lord."

Hattie followed Isurus away from the doors. His face was taut again, all the worry of earlier returned with double strength. "I will be to bed late," he said at last. "Please do not wait for me."

She reached up and kissed him gently. "If you need me, you know where to find me."

He pressed her hand in thanks and turned to leave. "Mokarran?"

"I will see her to her room." Mokarran inclined his body in a slight, proud bow.

The dark-eyed young man slid in step beside Hattie, silent as the moonlight. It was strange that they both knew Isurus so well, yet had barely said two words to one another.

They were nearly to the room when Hattie thought of something to say. "When will I get to meet your sister, Mokarran?"

He clasped his hands behind his back. "Soon. Her solitude is nearly over."

"I am sorry for her loss," Hattie said softly.

At this, the tall young man relaxed slightly. "It is the custom for our widows to remember the dead in solitude for a day and two nights. It is difficult to be alone when you are at the height of grief—"

For a moment, he fought to keep his mouth in its straight, proud line. Hattie's heart ached with understanding.

When he spoke, his voice was steady. "In the morning, no doubt, you shall meet her."

ELEVEN

Proto Aima

She was younger than Hattie expected. A fresh, girlish face, too pure for one to believe that she was in mourning, save for her eyes. Even their bright color—that of a clear sea in sunshine—could not hide the grief that lurked in them, just beyond the shallows.

But beneath her face was a pair of iron shoulders.

"Welcome to the House of Sphyrna and to the might of Atlantis," she greeted. "Long may the sun shine on you and your own."

Mokarran's sister pressed her hands together—her nails were colored with red pigment—and bowed. In that brief, still moment, the hot wind from the open gates caught the girl's light veil and whisked it back with her hair.

The image was burned into Hattie's memory: the maiden in mourning, standing in the courtyard of Sphyrna with a face like spring and the dignity of a queen.

She would not forget that image, she knew—not if seventy years rolled over it.

"I am grateful for the welcome, Zyaena." Hattie held out her hand. "And I am sorry."

A fierce look flashed in the girl's eyes, sad but strong. "Feel no sorrow for me. I aligned myself with a man of honor, and he met his end with honor. We ask no more of life."

"Even so, I am sorry that our return has interrupted your mourning."

Zyaena's face went soft, her features almost painfully sweet. "No…it is good that you have come. My brother and Crestus and

Isurus loved each other dearly. Mokarran wishes to be strong for me, but his own loss is great, and it does his heart more good than I can say to have Isurus by his side again."

Hattie followed the girl's gaze to where Mokarran stood, speaking with his steward, casting out his arm in demonstration of some order.

"He is too proud to show his grief," the girl murmured. "He wields more power than some kings, and yet I often feel the keenest need to protect him."

Hattie smiled. She knew the feeling.

"Now." Zyaena looked Hattie up and down. "Isurus says you have very little in the way of clothing."

Hattie was surprised that Isurus had given thought to anything to do with a woman's clothing, but he had surprised her often in the last few days.

"He's right."

"We shall have some made. The holding of memory for Crestus and the festival of the First Atlantean are both near at hand, and you must have clothes of your own. And jewelry. I can get the queen's jewels…Prionna has them locked away, but in another week, I will be back in her service, and I can take the key. She is not permitted to wear them, in any case."

"Is she not—?" Hattie felt suddenly shy and did not want to speak her thought out loud. She had thought that Prionna was Altimus's queen, or at least his betrothed.

Zyaena understood. "No. She and Altimus would never marry, even if they could. She is ambitious, and she pinned her ambition upon him…that is all. I will get the jewels." Zyaena glanced at Isurus, who was sitting nearby, and lowered her voice. "Isurus will be speechless when he sees you in his mother's jewels. He loved her."

"What was she like?"

"You should ask him." Zyaena's face darkened as she thought hard. "I do not remember her well. But I do remember that she was beautiful. And kind to me. I would have attended her as I do Prionna, if she had lived longer."

"Why are you in Prionna's service? If I may ask?"

Zyaena sighed, looking wise and weary beyond her years. "When Altimus came into the kingdom, Mokarran wanted nothing to do with him. If anyone can afford to give offense to the king, it is House Sphyrna…but I could not let my brother chance that. I serve the palace in his stead."

The sound of a stir out in the street arrested their attention. The day was hot, and the main gates of the house were open.

A shout sounded, close to the door.

Zyaena put her hand on Hattie's shoulder. "You cannot be seen."

Before Hattie had the chance to hide herself, Aeris ran in and was caught by the doorguard. His hair was wet, his tunic soaked through in places, as if he had been swimming and dressed in haste.

"It's Taurus."

Isurus started forward. "What happened?"

Aeris shook his head, gasping for breath.

Mokarran ran past him, out into the hot street. "Bring him here— no, there's isn't time! In here—send the healer here."

Isurus's face was very still. "Was it a shark?"

Aeris shook his wet hair out of his face. "We were in the runs, as we always are. One moment we were drilling, the next he was so taken with pains that he could not swim. I needed help to drag him out. They are carrying him, he's so doubled over—he cannot speak."

Isurus clenched his jaw. "It's poison, or I'm not a Lamnidae. This is my brother's doing."

"Quick!" Zyaena motioned for Isurus and Hattie to get out of sight just as the servants from the run came through the doors.

Hattie watched from behind the pillar as if in a dream. Mokarran never stopped giving terse orders as the servants ran to ready a room and Taurus appeared, carried by three men, doubled in pain, his fists clenched, his face twisted.

Isurus's voice broke through the dream, low and biting, nearly in her ear. "Heavens witness me, brother! You will answer for this."

"It took him less than a day. The fates were bound last night, and Taurus is dying by morning? Has he any fear?" Isurus's voice rang through the small room where they had taken refuge.

Hattie lingered near the door, hoping to catch the sound of the healer's voice from the next room. Aeris stood near the wall, listening silently to Isurus, rubbing his wrist below the golden armband that marked him as Master of War.

Mokarran started toward Isurus, his eyes dark with rage. "Did I not say, Isurus? He has grown dangerous. To stand in his way is to put a knife to your throat and to the throats of all who stand for you. Did I not say?"

Isurus stilled his friend with a hand on his arm. "Peace. You did."

"So you see, you cannot face him."

Isurus was quiet.

"Isurus. You cannot face him now. Without Taurus, he will learn soon enough."

"Silence. The healer says there is yet a chance."

"Just a chance, like the grasping of water. Oleander is swift."

"And Taurus is strong. If he lives—for his sake, I must face my brother." Isurus folded his arms. "And he will find it is much harder to kill me a second time."

A muscle twitched in Mokarran's cheek. "Swear you will do nothing without speaking to me first."

"My brother." Isurus's voice was gentle. "I will not hazard your throat lightly. You have my word."

Mokarran nodded. Beneath his hot temper, Hattie saw that he was strained and weary.

"The preparation for the holding of memory is not long off," he said, his voice low. "I will take my leave and send such food as will refresh you. Peace be on you."

Mokarran touched his shoulder briefly and went out.

Aeris pushed himself off the wall and bowed sharply in farewell.

Isurus halted him with a word. "What say you, Aeris? You have been with my brother."

Aeris glanced at the door that separated them from Taurus, his face stony, his eyes reluctant. "Your brother has grown in strength and becomes more ruthless with every victory. I say the sooner you strike, the sooner Atlantis is saved. And whatever else is done, we must be rid of Prionna."

He bowed again and left the room like a gust of wind.

Hattie gazed at the empty place where Aeris had stood, her mind still pondering the taut lines of his face. "Isn't he young to be charged with the fighting men of a whole kingdom?"

Isurus looked over at Hattie. His eyes gentled as if he had just remembered her presence. "He is nearly ten years my senior…and I am the king."

"Kings are born into things. He was chosen."

"He is competent." Isurus sagged onto the nearest couch, and Hattie went over and put her arms around him.

"It's going to be all right," she whispered, kissing him.

He leaned his head against hers without a word.

They turned toward the wide window that faced the water and sat together in silence, watching the daylight fade.

A servant brought in food and left it, but neither of them moved to get any.

They could not see the sun from the window, but Hattie's years at the lighthouse had taught her to know the sky. She guessed from the color of the light that the sun was just slipping beneath the sea when a voice—a thin, high, woman's voice—rose like a silver spire into the sky.

Alone it rose, spiraling gently upward in an ancient song.

"The songs of memory have begun," murmured Isurus. "So they prepare for the day of holding memory. The singing will last until the dawn."

"What is she saying?"

"*Nolitae desperar*—do not lose hope." His voice was rough with emotion. "Do not lose hope, for after death comes life, after loss comes gain, and old harms pass like forgotten fears into the night. Dawn swallows all with joy."

Hattie breathed out, the words falling on her heart like sweet relief. "Are all Atlantean songs so beautiful?"

"Most of them."

The single voice was joined by a host—dozens out on the grounds were singing.

"Do not lose hope," Hattie whispered.

They heard a sudden cry from the next room, and Isurus cringed.

"He's fighting," he said, as if to give himself courage.

The song changed—a lament this time. "To the cold stars," Isurus said, but offered nothing more.

The door opened. Isurus got swiftly to his feet. It was one of the healer's apprentices.

"How is he?"

But the boy only shook his head and hastened on his errand. He returned a few minutes later, followed by servants bearing hot water and odd-smelling compounds.

The door shut with a dull thud, and Isurus dropped his head into his hands.

"I should have foreseen this. Taurus is wild, but he has a good heart, and I have always been hard on him. If he dies—"

"Dearest, don't think." Hattie could not let him go on like that. "Nothing can be gained by it now. Just rest."

The singing rose again, a swift-tongued song with longing in the rise and fall of the music. Hattie leaned her head against Isurus's chest, and he reached his long arms around her. The beat of his heart was strong and comforting, and with the music in her ears and the stars in her gaze, she slipped into sleep.

She woke with a start as Isurus stirred.

Through bleary eyes, she saw the door to Taurus's room had been opened and the healer stood in the doorway.

The night was wearing thin.

"He has asked for you, sovereignty."

Isurus started up, gently moving his arm out from under her. Wearily she stood and followed him to where the healer stood, haggard and gray around the eyes.

"He will live. But he may be in some pain for the day."

"You will be rewarded, healer." Isurus's voice was thick.

"No reward is needed, my lord. Be calm when you speak to him; his body is weary from fighting. I will go lie down a spell, within call."

"We will be brief and quiet."

Hattie followed Isurus into the dim room, where a single sheltered candle burned in one corner.

Taurus lay on the bed with his head against the headrest, his eyes wandering to their faces as they entered.

"Dear cousin." Isurus spoke softly. "The healer tells me you are as stubborn as old Phaedius."

The ghost of a smile tempered the weary glint of Taurus's eyes. A matter of hours had left him vastly changed. He was drawn, his face almost skeletal, his jaw tilted up like someone on the edge of deep pain. He was slick with sweat.

"I am glad you are here." His voice, too, was thin.

"I would be nowhere else." Isurus took his cousin's hand. "I was afraid all night that I would never again look upon your face like this."

"You were a fool to worry," Taurus whispered.

"Yes," Isurus agreed, glancing down and away to hide his tears.

"I am…very tired," Taurus murmured weakly. "But I would that you stayed a little longer."

"Sleep. I will remain here for as long as you wish it." Isurus settled on the ground beside Taurus's low bed and kept his grip on his cousin's hand.

After a few minutes, Hattie slipped out, leaving them together.

A thin band of gold lay across the horizon between the sea and the night sky, spreading pale dawn around it. A new song had started, slow and reverent and wildly beautiful. *Resurgam aurora*, they were singing—arise, dawn.

Hattie leaned her chin on her hand and watched as the sun rose from the sea and the song swelled with the golden light, growing stronger and more triumphant as the warm rays spread over the sea and flooded the white walls behind her.

Arise, dawn! Bring hope to life, and fling death to the depths of the sea.

In the beginning, the words of the lies were sweet.

They came easier than the truth, most times: fair words, words of lasting allegiance, hiding what he thought behind a pleasing mask. But the more they were believed, the more he despised those who believed them. It drove him mad, seeing their mild acceptance of his falsehoods, and something inside him roared to be let free—to show them, just once, who he really was, what he really thought of them.

He told her how he felt once, and she gave him an understanding look.

"Is it any wonder that the gods cannot live among men? It is because they would not be able to abide it. Take heart. One day we too shall rise, and we will be forced to live among them no longer."

Those words were what kept him sane.

TWELVE

Meet Me to My Face

"It is customary to wear white," said Zyaena. "For most everyone."

Hattie watched quietly as Mokarran's sister brought out the dress, made in a single day, and laid it on a chair.

A long, heated discussion between Isurus and his three advisors that morning had ended in the decision that Isurus and Hattie would make their arrival known to Atlantis at the holding of memory for Crestus.

Mokarran, particularly, had been against it.

Zyaena brought out a large bracelet and a heavy pair of gold earrings. "These will do well. And your hair—you will let it down."

Hattie unpinned her hair and let it cascade down her back. Her mother had always spoken with pride of the thick hair the women of her family had, inherited from some great-grandmother who came over from the old country.

"Thank you for doing this." Hattie reached out and put a hand over Zyaena's. She remembered how she had felt the morning of her mother's funeral, and the afternoon of Jack's. The girl's quietness moved her.

Zyaena gave a small shake of her head. "Go. Put those on, and I will see what else can be done."

When Hattie had changed, Zyaena led her with an almost childish delight to a mirror that stood in the corner. The woman who stared back from the mirror was almost a stranger to Hattie.

"I will get out my paints…we shall put a little ebony on your eyes. You shall look like a queen indeed." Zyaena's smile stiffened slightly.

"And that will make Altimus jealous."

"Why does he have no queen?"

"I suppose he could find one…but marriage in Atlantis is very binding, and the women very fierce." She brought her jar of paints and began to edge Hattie's eyes with fine, deft strokes. "One does well to choose slowly and carefully, lest he wake with a knife in his back. Or not wake, as it may be."

She spoke casually, with no hint of humor or exaggeration. Hattie was shocked into silence.

"Hold still." Zyaena pressed her lips together as she concentrated. Then a dimple appeared in one cheek. "Isurus will never forgive me if I put your eye out."

Isurus spread the ash upon her forehead with his own thumb, all the while staring at her in wonder. He had crowned her with the customary circlet of a lord's wife, but in his eyes, she saw that he was thinking of a later crown.

He wore a long white kilt with a net of woven gold draped about his waist and chest and great bands of gold around his arms. They lent a savagery but also a dignity to his bearing, as if he was born to look this way.

"My *starra*," he whispered when he was done. And for once, she didn't know what he meant.

Mokarran was dressed as Isurus's double, revealing the dark tattoo of a stingray that spanned his back and shoulders. A warning to his enemies, he told Hattie, for the stingray was the favorite prey of hammerhead sharks.

Zyaena alone wore black, which made her seem pale and ten feet tall and distant as the night.

Dressed as they were in their ancient finery, with ash on their proud faces, Hattie could not help but feel that whatever happened in the future, they were untouchable tonight.

The golden light of the sun bathed the white walls of the palace, turning them to brilliant gold. The sea, too, had changed its coat for the ceremony, moving like liquid metal from a smith's mold.

Outside, emerging from all corners of the palace, people were moving in silence, their feet echoing on the stone, every man and woman dressed in white and gold with smears of ash on their faces.

Hattie saw Aeris and Galeio, both solemn-faced, moving in a sea of strangers.

"There," Isurus whispered in her ear. "My brother and Prionna."

Across the stones strode a bearded man, head and shoulders above those around him. Brindled hair hung to his shoulders, and his eyebrows rose like hawk's wings above dark, lionlike eyes. Like all the others, he was dressed in white, but the blue tattoo on his shoulder was bared, and the blue of state hung across his broad chest. Beside him glided a small, slim woman with thick dark hair and steel-blue eyes, her head carried high upon her slim neck and shoulders.

For a fleeting moment, Hattie could see it.

They were heroes, with a mist of destiny hanging about them that she with her Maine sturdiness and Isurus with his quiet manner could never match.

Then she remembered Taurus as they had left him, haggard and racked with pain, and all their beauty faded.

As if he could feel their eyes, Altimus turned his head. Hattie felt as though caught in a bad dream as the dark gaze came to rest on Isurus.

Isurus's fingers parted from hers, quietly distancing himself.

His brother's face went a strange shade, darker than before. His eyes were like coals, his lips parted in a silent snarl. Beside him, Prionna looked up, and her pure, proud look dissolved in quiet disbelief.

Then Isurus stepped into the procession of men and Hattie followed the women, and Altimus and Prionna were lost in the silent sweep of the parting company.

Just ahead of Hattie, dark amid the white-clad figures, walked Zyaena, the gold of her circlet shining as bright as the dying sun. She marched at the center of the men like the eye of a storm, while the other women drew back and waited.

A woman, passing by, handed Hattie a white candle and lit it with her own. "Blessings on you for your compassion on those beyond the sun," she said in a tone of benediction, then moved on to the next woman.

When the men had passed, the women fell in behind them. The flagstones beneath their feet were still warm from the afternoon sun as they passed through the city and came to a silent halt on the edge of the sea.

The sun, sinking behind the waves, took Hattie's breath away. It was no longer the warm, distant presence she knew from her northern climate, but a king, rising and falling into the sea with the vigor of an athlete. The sea, too, had a life of its own—a quietness, like it was biding its time, far different from the reckless abandon of the sea in Maine.

Mokarran stood at the center of it all, the men on one side of him and the women on the other, and Zyaena at his side. A white bird wheeled in the sky above.

Isurus was lost to her sight.

The wind was ruffling Mokarran's straight black hair, playing gently like a child that does not know to mourn, the sun kissing his face gently like a warm embrace at the end of a day full of joy.

He lifted his head, his face to the setting sun, and began a solemn song.

"As the sun goes down to the sea and the seas return to the springs where they were born, so we bid you go, go with the sun, and to joys unknown."

"Farewell, farewell," answered the crowd in unison, and Hattie joined in with the women around her: "We shall meet on the dawn."

"As the great sharks come to feed and leave again and return in their season with young, so we say farewell for a time, for in the dawn we shall be with you also."

"Farewell, farewell," echoed the crowd. "We shall meet on the dawn."

"And so farewell, and so farewell!" Mokarran's voice grew louder and seemed to fill the air around them like a great defiance to the silence of the heavens above. "To the golden city shall we go and in the dawn meet one another again. And so farewell."

"We shall laugh, we shall feast, we shall forget griefs forever in a river of beauty," answered the crowd. "And so farewell!"

The Lord of the Shark Kind, dressed in white, with no ash on his marble-like face, came forward, holding fast a young shark—a slim thing, perhaps two feet long, its gray skin streaked with blue, the color of joy.

Zyaena took the young shark carefully from his hands and walked down the steps alone to the sea. Her skirt caught the water and floated gently about her as she lowered the creature to the haven of the seawater. "On the dawn we shall meet," she said, and released the animal.

The shark writhed away in a rush of foam and bubbles, then eased into the clear water, skimming away with a gentle flick of its tail.

"And so farewell!" cried the men, raising their spears with a great shout. The women moved forward as one, and Hattie was caught up in the moment, her limbs obeying as if she had done this her entire life. They all knelt beside the water, extinguishing their flames in the sea.

A great hiss rose, and thin, acrid smoke hovered above the sea for a moment before the gentle breeze carried it away.

Zyaena had flowers now, a great armful; and she threw them out over the sea.

Mokarran turned to the throng. "It is done. Long live the memory of the one who dies in honor."

"Long live the memory of the one who dies in honor!" the throng cried back, as one.

It was growing dark by the time Hattie found Isurus. His face was set like steel, only changing long enough for him to give a brief smile of acknowledgement as he took her hand. He did not need to say a word; she knew he wanted to return to Mokarran's house as quickly as possible.

When they reached the square at the entrance to the palace grounds, where the great houses were situated, Isurus stopped.

Altimus stood waiting for them, Prionna watching from his shadow.

The look in the woman's eyes sat like lead in Hattie's stomach.

Altimus seemed even larger now that Hattie stood before him; he was tall and muscular, his eyes golden like a lion's, and his lip curled in a snarling smile.

With a soft clank, Isurus laid his hand upon his gold-netted chest.

"Good health, Altimus," he greeted, every word a splinter of steel.

The greeting seemed to rouse Altimus from his ruminations. A broad white smile spread in his dark, gleaming beard, accentuating a scar that ran down his cheek and kissed the edge of one eyebrow.

But the reply he gave was a wordless growl.

"Taurus lives." Hattie had never heard Isurus's voice so cold and clear. "Your oleander was wasted on him, for it was me you sought. I have returned, and the fates are bound because there cannot be two anointed kings of Atlantis."

"My brother." Altimus's voice was rich, but the words sounded sharp and bitter on his tongue. "You were condemned as a lawbreaker and an outcast. You forsook the ancient laws of our people, and just punishment was meted to you. You were forbidden to return."

Isurus's laugh rang loud and clear in the darkening square.

"The sea was my judge, and atonement was paid me upon my return. Graciously, I forgave the trespass of my people. And now I return and demand my right—the crown."

"It is no longer your right. Your life you have, your throne you lost."

"And would the Lord of the Shark Kind make a mistake?"

Altimus stepped right into the trap.

"No, the Lord of the Shark Kind is just in all his ways, as he was when he anointed me king after your disgrace."

"The Lord of the Shark Kind anointed me challenger-king the very night I stepped foot in Atlantis, and you, coming on my heels, sought his counsel only to find the fates bound. My dear brother, you know there is only one course before you."

"Altimus, come away." Prionna spoke for the first time, her voice low and strong but velvet-soft. "We will settle with your brother in time."

But her eyes were on Hattie's face.

Altimus stepped forward, closing the gap between them. He leaned into Isurus's face—they were nearly the same height, but Altimus was twice as broad. "You will die in disgrace, Isurus. And I will enjoy seeing you do it a second time."

"A diver puts his hand into the den of a cave-shark but once."

The proverb must have been answer enough, for Altimus's eyes flicked over to Hattie. "And what is this?"

"The queen, Altimus. Hail her, the only queen of Atlantis."

It cost Hattie no effort at all to stare daggers into the man's wild golden eyes. After all the pain she had been forced to witness—Isurus, Taurus, Mokarran, Zyaena—she felt almost eager to let him see how little she thought of him.

And then, surprising even herself, she smiled at him. "You heard the king."

"Challenger-king, sweet lady," he growled through his teeth. "There must be a king for there to be a challenger. And I am he."

"If you are truly king," she replied, keeping her voice low and steady, "then you have nothing to fear from a challenger."

A slow smile slid up Altimus's face. "I like her, Isurus. Keep her."

Nothing else had penetrated Isurus's calm, but at this remark, Hattie felt him stiffen. "I have said what I mean to say, brother." His voice was brittle. "But let one last thing stand between us."

The two men's faces were lit in the darkness by the eerie light of their glowing tattoos. Hattie's heart pulsed in her throat.

"I will not be taken as Crestus and Taurus were taken. I have daggers in the shadows. Meet me to my face, or meet me not at all."

THIRTEEN

The Promise of a Liar

"Prionna is the one you must watch. She is more dangerous than a reef shark." Mokarran folded his arms and leaned against the fountain. "If I was to lay a wager, I would say we will have a response from her this very morning."

Isurus laughed grimly. "Wager on the hour?"

Mokarran opened his mouth to speak.

"Do not wager," warned Zyaena, lifting her chin from her hand. She was as composed as ever, but seemed weary. Hattie had hardly heard her speak five words together this morning.

It was cool in the shadows, but the morning sun was already hot on the pavement, promising a scorching day. Breakfast was laid in the courtyard at Mokarran's request, and the four of them ranged slowly around it, like sharks through a school of fish.

"How is Taurus this morning?" asked Hattie, plucking a date from one of the vast plates.

Isurus ran his fingers through his dark hair. "Pale as a ghost, but he'll be on his feet before long. By the feast, I would imagine."

"It's little more than a week hence." Mokarran raised an eyebrow. "And if—"

A thunderous pounding came at the door. All four of them exchanged sharp glances.

"That is no pleasant visitor come to discuss the rain and the tides, or I miss my mark," said Isurus dryly.

Mokarran called for a servant to answer, and Hattie took a step nearer to Isurus. No one moved to continue eating.

Isurus craned his neck to see the visitor through the doors. "Looks like a Black Tip. You were right, Mokarran. It has come, and sooner than I thought."

Mokarran's man came hurrying back to address Isurus. "It is a messenger from the king. He wishes to have words with you, sovereign."

"Is he alone?"

"He has a single guard."

"Not Stellarus?"

Hattie caught a glance exchanged between Mokarran and his sister. Whoever Stellarus was, he was not to be trusted.

"No, sovereignty."

"Let them come."

The messenger and the guard came forward. The guard, dressed in black and gold, was tall and broad through the shoulders, but rangy. His hair was closely cropped, and his nose jutted like that of a shark.

Isurus rose to meet them. "What would you have with me?"

"The Shark King, Altimus Carcharodon, Lord of the Sun Throne, ruler of Atlantis and the surrounding seas, does greet you, saying that he has been pleased to behold your face and will be pleased to behold it again; and in assurance of his gracious temper and goodwill, he sends you this gift."

The messenger stepped aside, and the guard, dressed in the black and gold of the Black Tips, came forward and bowed his forehead to the ground.

"Yours to command, my lord."

A turn of speech, Hattie suspected, rather than the truth.

"I am sent as a gift from my lord, Altimus Carcharodon, for your protection, as surety that no attempt shall be made upon your life until such time as the laws declare combat or a like decision."

Isurus studied the man.

"My brother mocks me. Poison, I would have thought, would be his choice. Or an assassin, perhaps, swift and silent. You are not a gift, but a mockery. An assurance that he can protect my life or take it from me at a word."

The man remained bowed on the hot pavement, motionless.

"Rise," Isurus said at last. He looked the man up and down. "You have long been in my brother's service, am I not right? You are Vulpinus Alopias."

"My lord speaks true."

"And what say you to entering the service of the challenger-king? The enemy of your lord?"

"I say nothing." Vulpinus swallowed, his eyes fixed straight ahead. "I only obey what duty is expected of me."

"Tell me, how was my brother to you? Remember, I am your lord now."

The man was quiet a moment. "He was good to me, and just."

"A cruel man may yet treat his dogs well."

Hattie felt a deep misgiving. She saw the moment Isurus began to relent, and she opened her mouth to warn him against it, but he spoke too swiftly. "You will find me fair. Come, Vulpinus, I will give you house-room."

Vulpinus bowed in thanks.

Mokarran was no more pleased than Hattie. He glowered darkly at Vulpinus over the rim of his cup. "If you betray him, I will make you wish you were never born. With my own two hands I'll do it."

The guard's response was nearly emotionless. "If it will set your lordship's mind at ease, I took the *carum-inum* before I came."

"It will not hurt you to take it again, in our hearing." Mokarran stepped forward almost into the man's face, an almost savage look in his proud eyes.

The guard stood his ground.

Isurus shook his head mildly. "It's a blood oath, Mokarran. If he's done it, there is a cut on his wrist."

Mokarran's hand shot out and caught the man's wrist, turning it up to the light. A small bloodstained bandage lay under his armguard.

"He could have cut it himself. Or more likely, Altimus had it done. He may not have sworn the oath at all."

"I did it, by Nalak," said the guard. "But since you insist—"

His lip curled into a sneer. He reached into a sheath strapped to his leg and unbuckled the armguard, making a nick across his bare forearm. He turned it over and let the blood drip onto the floor.

"By the sun, by the ancient laws, by our brothers who rule the sea, I swear to keep my oath. I will guard my lord, Isurus Lamnidae, to the death, and no harm will I bring upon him from this day until the world's end, unless he release me from this oath. Should I break faith, may the seas rise to cover me, the sun fall to burn me, and the mountains come to crush me. May my lord find this oath pleasing in his eyes."

The ease with which the man swore such drastic oaths alarmed Hattie, but Isurus nodded as though talk of the sun falling was perfectly ordinary. "I accept this oath. Go, and get that arm seen to."

Vulpinus turned to obey, and suddenly a cry tore through the room.

"Traitor! Bait for sharks!"

A young woman, clad in purple and blazing gold, came striding across the courtyard toward Vulpinus, brandishing a wicked-looking knife.

"My lord?" Vulpinus looked uncertainly at Isurus, his knife loose in his fingers.

"Hold," Isurus ordered softly.

Mokarran set down his goblet, leaping forward. "My lady!"

"Traitor! Ingrate! Dog!" the woman shouted, drowning him out. "Dare you draw your weapon on the true king?"

Isurus rose. "Tryaena—"

"Tryaena!" Mokarran seized her arm as she lunged at Vulpinus. "He is my lord's hound now."

"He is a Black Tip. They do not change their colors," she spat.

"Nevertheless, Isurus has given him house-room. Pray, do not knife him on my grounds."

Tryaena tossed the hair out of her face and fixed the guard with a stare like death. She was small, but her eyes gleamed viciously. Hattie had no doubt that this woman was capable of carrying out her threats. "Have a care, snake, that I do not part your head from your writhing body."

Vulpinus eyed her slowly and then reached down, his eyes still trained on her face, to sheath his knife. The blood ran from his cut, dripping off the tips of his fingers.

"Go see to your arm." Isurus waved him away to safety with an almost imperceptible gesture. "She won't touch you."

Vulpinus stiffened as if insulted and left.

"My lady Tryaena." Isurus came forward, holding out his hand. "Do sheath your zealous knife and greet your king."

Tryaena jerked her arm from Mokarran's grasp and spit contemptuously on the floor. The knife spun in her fingers as her eyes lit on Hattie. She stared at her for a long moment, spinning the knife before she returned it to its sheath with a slow scrape.

Then she bowed to Isurus with her fist pressed to her shoulder, the sun illuminating her red hair. "Sovereignty, I resent that I was not told of your arrival sooner. Surely no heart has more zeal for your kingdom than mine."

Isurus spread his hands in a gesture of peace. "I have only just come."

"And that dog was in your house before I was."

"He is under my protection." A sterner note entered Isurus's voice. "Swear to me you won't hurt him."

Tryaena looked up with quiet resentment. "Sometimes my lord does not choose wisely for himself."

"He swore the *carum-inum*."

The woman let her breath out slowly. "I will make him eat every word of it when he betrays you."

"If he betrays me," corrected Isurus gently. "Now tell me, how stands the House of Carcharhinus?"

"If you think that he will not betray you," said Tryaena softly, ignoring his last question, "then you did not learn well enough the first time."

Vulpinus's tall shoulders briefly blocked the beating sun, and Hattie adjusted her step to keep him between her and the sun.

In the week that followed his appointment, he had been nothing but obedient to Isurus's orders, and today, as Hattie returned early from a meeting with the lords of the port she had attended with Isurus, he accompanied her home with strict instructions regarding her safety.

"You will be within the sight of many until you reach Mokarran's house," Isurus had assured her. "And the *carum-inum* is a fearful oath. You are safer with him than without him."

Hattie still did not trust the man, but she had no immediate fear that he would try anything violent. Whatever Altimus and Prionna intended, they were keeping it to themselves for the time being.

As if in answer to her thoughts, she saw Prionna, coming down the road the opposite way. She wore white, as she had in the square; her hair was bound in a thick braid over her shoulder, and a gold chain hung across her forehead.

She looked like a queen.

For a moment, Hattie thought that Prionna would ignore her existence, but instead the woman drew aside.

"Afternoon," Hattie greeted, her voice deliberately frigid.

"Are you afraid of me?" Prionna's mouth curved—not quite a smile.

"No." Hattie almost laughed. She certainly was not.

"Naturally not." Prionna's gaze flicked to Vulpinus, and something in her look made Hattie uneasy.

"Do you want something?"

Prionna raised her chin proudly and looked down her nose. "I hear you are not only a foreign bride, but from across the great Atlantic sea."

"I am."

"I too, was born elsewhere." She let out her breath as her gaze swept the open, hot sky. "Atlantis is quite dizzying when you are not used to it."

"I hadn't noticed." Hattie folded her arms. "Now what is it you want? I don't flatter myself that you're here to exchange pleasantries."

Prionna looked her directly in the eyes. "Your husband is not an honorable man. I don't know what lies he told you to bring you here, but his promises are empty."

"The promises he made me are no more empty here than they were in my country."

Prionna gave a gentle laugh. "I do not think you understand. You did not know him growing up. He was weak, he was petty; his best quality was his face. Better suited to that flame-haired girl of Carcharhinus, though I don't suppose you know her. She wouldn't be pleased to know about you."

"We met." Hattie's voice was calm, but she could feel her blood begin to heat.

Prionna raised her eyebrows. "Be careful—she might knife you for him."

"Since you plotted against my husband's life and crown, I hardly think you are the person I should be taking advice from."

Prionna's eyes were hard. "Altimus only took the throne—as his right—after your husband committed a crime so low that even his status as king could not save him."

She wasn't worth answering.

"Come, Vulpinus." Hattie started off across the paving stones. "I wish to be out of the sun."

"From woman to woman," Prionna said to Hattie's back, "leave him before he sinks you with the rest of Atlantis. The moment his life is threatened, he will crush you to save himself. You should have stayed in your own land across the sea. At least a girl like Tryaena would be able to stand up against him—for you, there will be no hope once he is driven by fear."

Hattie rounded on her. "You will not tell me my business with my husband, is that understood?" It was the tone a member of the Ladies'

Aid Society might have used on a drunken boatman, and she was shocked to hear it coming out of her own mouth.

"A word of warning." Prionna's voice was like ice. "If your husband does not step back, he will not only die, he will die in infamy, amid the greatest dishonor Atlantis has ever known."

"I thought you tried that already."

The air was still and hot around them.

"You are out of your depth." Prionna smiled. It could almost have been sweet. "What makes you think he will succeed this time, without the protection of the throne?"

"I want you to understand one thing." Hattie took her time, measured her words one by one. "Last time, he didn't have me. And I may not be much, but I intend to put up one whale of a fight."

Prionna's full lips curved into a smile, but her eyes were bitter.

"Good. We know where we stand, then."

They were jeweled like a sunken Spanish galleon, the *luxarmum*—great collars of metal, stretching from just below the jaw to the waistline, studded with blue and white jewels, line upon line, like the endless waves on a shore.

"Isurus, I can hardly move. How are we supposed to do anything?"

"We needn't do anything, save eat and sing." He stood at the curtained window, looking down over the hall below. "Once a year, we all wear them. To honor our forefathers and remind us that pride will bring destruction."

"Somehow, I don't think all this extravagance helps in the area of pride." Hattie tilted her neck and grimaced.

Isurus let the curtain fall. "You look beautiful, my dearest."

"Flattery won't work."

"I did not say it would." He leaned down a little stiffly, his armlet clanking against her bejeweled shoulder, and kissed the top of her head. "I will be the first to admit, on behalf of my people, that we are imperfect. But who am I to tell thousands of years of tradition that I beg exception?"

Hattie yielded to the inevitable and leaned her head against his hard shoulder.

In the still moment, she could hear the hum of voices below.

"Will there be many people here tonight?"

"Yes. Most of the palace and some of the merchants." Isurus went to the window and drew back the curtain slightly. "See?"

The distinct smell of honey-wine and warm perfume rose from below them, where a sea of glittering people milled. For the barest moment, Hattie wished desperately for the smell of her own familiar gatherings: coffee, salt, damp wool, lobster and pie and hot bread.

"What is the matter?"

"Nothing."

"Hattie?" He was worried, wanted to fix whatever was wrong.

"I was just thinking of the gatherings at home. How different they are." *How much less dangerous.*

"I'm sorry."

"And why should you be? Sorry that we love each other? Sorry that I want to be with you so much I would leave my home for yours? I don't see anything to be sorry about."

He caught her fingers in his. "Are you ready?"

She clasped his hand warmly in reply.

They kept to themselves at first, mingling more to be seen than to speak, discussing what they saw in undertones. Vulpinus followed them like an unpleasant shadow, just out of whispered earshot.

Prionna was similarly reserved, following Altimus quietly as he laughed and talked and charmed his way around the room, only whispering in his ear now and then. Her *luxarmum* was of stunning green and silver, and she wore a bracelet that wound its way up her arm like a snake. Watching them, Hattie had to admit that Altimus—if you left out the scheming and the killing—was the kind of man one expected to be king. Loud and warm and hearty.

"Is it true that Prionna was not born in Atlantis?" she asked Isurus in an undertone, wresting her gaze from their rivals.

"It is true. She, like Altimus, is half Carmian."

"What is that?"

"They are from the west. Beautiful and strong and hot-blooded. But her father dedicated her to Sol, which means she can never marry."

"Do Atlanteans do that? Dedicating your child to gods—"

"No, it is a thing that is done by Carmians."

"And she had no say in it?"

"Of course not. It was done when she was a baby. But I don't think she has ever much desired marriage. And as for being a servant of Sol—well, I'm not sure that there's anything to that."

Prionna lifted her head at that moment and laughed. There was something wild in that laugh.

"I think she's happy as she is." Isurus's voice sounded sad.

A throat cleared behind them, and Hattie saw Galeio, a silver goblet in his hand. "Good evening." He bowed to them both.

"Galeio, my friend! How fares Atlantis?"

A distant smile passed over the man's face.

"Your presence betters it, that much is clear. The lords are nearly in your hand, I think. I have spoken to many of them, even in the last seven days, and your innocence is proof enough to them."

"I will drink to that." Isurus lifted his goblet in salute. Galeio took only a discreet sip from his.

"Do you see that guard?" Galeio leaned close to Hattie, nodding toward a tall fellow in the livery of the Black Tips. He reminded Hattie of the Greek heroes from her father's book of myths, with curly dark hair and a sweet, cupid's bow curve to his mouth.

"The one who's missing a hand?"

"Yes. A shark did that. He was one of the Kind…an apprentice. But if a shark maims you like that, you're cast out. Dangerous with a knife, he is."

The man was much older than Isurus, but he had a youthful face, with a pleasantness about it that settled on Hattie's stomach like too much rich cake.

"His name's Stellarus. A piece of advice. If you see him, walk the other way."

Spoken in Galeio's smooth, easy tone, the words chilled her to her marrow. She suddenly felt that the whole room was full of potential enemies.

She looked up to thank Galeio for his advice, but he was gone.

"It is time for the ceremony," whispered Isurus. "Come."

They crossed the room to where Mokarran stood, at the very head of the throng, and held out their goblets.

A servant poured out honey-wine, a few mouthfuls each.

A hush fell upon the gathering, and from their midst appeared the Lord of the Shark Kind, the crowd parting for him like water.

He lifted a goblet, finer than the rest—silver and blue, like the *luxarmum* of Lamnidae—and held it aloft.

"Drink," he ordered, grim and deep.

Solemnly Isurus lifted his glass to his lips, and Hattie followed suit.

"Do you taste life?" asked the Lord of the Shark Kind.

"We taste," replied a hundred voices or more, Isurus's voice strong beside Hattie.

"Do you remember?"

"Our ancestors were proud and paid for it with destruction," answered the throng.

"Only by grace did we survive, through one man," continued the Lord of the Shark Kind.

"Woe, woe to the proud," said the people, "and those raised high."

"So we remember that doom comes to the proud and pray that it passes over us."

The people echoed this.

"Let honor and peace grace us," said the throng with finality. A servant came to them with a bowl of salt, and Isurus sprinkled a pinch in the last swallow of their wine.

"Sweet to salt," said the people, and they drank.

For the space of a dozen heartbeats, profound silence reigned. Then the room seemed to let out a sigh, and the murmur of celebration washed back in like a tide. Isurus smiled, taking Hattie's cup.

"It is over," he said. "Now we eat, we sing, and all shall be well. We will go to the gardens of Sphyrna for the feast."

Already people were moving that way, heading out into the fading day, down a great flight of steps to the cool, fresh air below.

The gardens had quickly become one of Hattie's favorite places, surrounded by rows of cool trees and lush hedges, crossed with canals and dotted with pools full of fish, bursting with bright flowers and plants of deep hues she would never have seen in Maine. The rich scent of the flowers rose to meet the heady perfumes and the sweet smell of new wine until Hattie's senses were almost overpowered.

"Doom!" cried a voice, a woman's, breaking through the dusk, halting the people in their steps, dropping the pleasant murmur of conversation to an uncomfortable silence.

Isurus went white. "No," he whispered, so softly that only Hattie could have caught it in the still air.

Prionna was climbing, mounting the pedestal of a great statue at the top of the steps to the hall, her thick dark hair loose and swinging behind her back. The *luxarmum* was gone, her white dress gleaming in the dusk.

"Doom comes upon Atlantis!" she cried as she reached the height of it, standing above the people. They all stood frozen in frightened wonder.

The torchlight that lined the garden paths was only just overtaking the dim light, but up on the pedestal of the statue, the last of the day's light lit her face with its pale reflection.

"Wise and worthy people of Atlantis, hear the words which I speak now!"

Hattie heard Isurus's breath go out of him quietly.

"Is it not written in the Book of the Blessed that 'he who follows his own path and regards not the laws and pronouncements of the wise, he is doomed'? And is it not also written that a doomed man brings doom upon his house, and the greater the man, the greater the fall?"

There was a heavy silence; not so much in disagreement, Hattie thought, but in fearful fascination.

"Is it not so?"

There was a murmur of assent from the people.

"And if the man's house be the whole of Atlantis, what then? If he is doomed, will he not bring the whole of it down?"

There was a gasp, and Prionna threw her head back in response to it, her face proud and terrible. She had the people where she wanted them.

"As it has been written,

In the season of the running of the blued fish,

under the stars of Achilles,

portents will come, and after memory's holding

the Doom will be revealed.

"Are we not under the stars of Achilles?"

There was a murmur of assent from the people.

"Were not the blued fish seen again, running in our waters, as they have not since the days of our fathers' fathers?"

The murmurs were no longer of agreement only; the crowd's response took on a fearful tone.

"And are there not portents that have newly fallen upon us?"

The crowd fell into a silence worse than the fearful murmurs.

"Behold, the Doom of Atlantis!" she shouted, casting her hand toward Isurus. "He has brought these evils and tremors of the earth upon our kingdom! The sharks are thinning, the halls beneath the sea quake, the Shark Kind are silent in their premonitions. You see before you the one who will be the destruction of his people if he is not first destroyed!"

Isurus dropped Hattie's hand and strode forward, up the stairs toward the statue.

The crowd parted, leaving a wide path for him. Prionna watched him approach with the eagerness of a hawk.

He mounted the steps and reached up as if to give her a hand. "Prionna, for the love of Atlantis, please come down. You know not of what you speak, nor is it your place to sow fear in the hearts of the people. They must be protected."

Prionna looked down at him and laughed. "Fear twists your face, O outcast."

"I fear nothing." He said it loud enough that the calm, clean sense could be heard by all. "Nor does Atlantis have anything to fear."

"Oh, but so should speak the Doom!" laughed Prionna. "For it is written in the wise teachings of the ancients that the Doom of Atlantis, he from whom the Last Atlantean shall deliver his people, will do his own will and not that of the land, nor of the sea, nor of the Brotherhood, and shall strive to deceive his people that they are safe from him."

"Prionna, this spectacle is not right," Isurus insisted. "Nor should such words be spoken after those of ceremony. Come down."

"Even now, the Doom brings danger upon his people!" Prionna cried, casting her hand down at him. "With every hour he yet threatens us by his presence. Atlantis shakes at his coming! I warn you, people of Atlantis!"

As if in answer to Prionna, a shudder ran through the earth. Screams tore the air—a horrible sound. Then the ground began to shake, almost lifting beneath her feet.

Isurus abandoned Prionna, running back to Hattie. His hand gripped hers, pulling her away from the crumbling stone.

"Quick, Hattie—stay with me."

She glanced back, once.

The people were divided, half of them fleeing, half of them cowering in terror. And Prionna was still perched on the statue, fearless, crying doom to them all.

It was a thing he had once heard said: no man, in the end, wants to die alone.

The phrase had clung to him like a wet garment all day—the day he should have been gladdest. The death of one's enemies should make the heart glad.

And he was glad. Had he not grown to hate the brother he sent away alone?

Yet he had drowned everything in the feasting wine that night and dreamed of green waves.

FOURTEEN

Behold, the Doom

A small flame lit the near-silent courtyard in the center of the hall, casting hard shadows on the empty, ragged floor.

The feast had been abandoned after the earthquake, the people fleeing home. It had not lasted long, and the destruction was not serious, but the damage had been done.

Across the brazier from Hattie stood Galeio, who had only just returned from the palace, a white-faced Aeris in his wake. Neither looked like they had slept.

Mokarran had sent for Isurus and now stood watching the fire, arms folded, the light of the flames playing in his dark eyes.

"What is it?" asked Isurus, appearing from an inner room. Broken stone and plaster ground beneath his feet.

"It goes ill." Galeio's blue eyes were miserable. "I would rather strike off my hand than be the bearer of this, sovereignty." He held out a sealed scroll.

Isurus took the scroll from Galeio's ringed fingers, his eyes still on the man's face. He broke the seal and read silently.

"So. For the good of Atlantis, I am *ana-timeth?*"

Galeio lowered his eyes and nodded.

Mokarran made an ugly sound in his throat.

"And what is this?" Isurus smacked the open parchment with the back of his hand. "The Doom is born under the constellation of Odysseus? She has gall to be naming my birth stars so."

Galeio's face gave a strange twist. "It is in the Book of the Blessed. It is not of her invention."

Isurus lowered the parchment silently. "You mean it, don't you?"

"I would die thrice over before I would lie to you, sovereignty, though doing so would be easier than causing you pain."

Isurus swallowed and lifted the parchment again, reading carefully.

"So it is," he said at last, his voice a little shaky.

Hattie looked over his shoulder. The language was thick and traveling, but Hattie gathered that *ana-timeth* meant forbidden or outcast. The constellation nonsense was clear enough.

Mokarran snatched the parchment from his friend's hands and read over it himself. "The dog, the *dog!*"

He turned on Galeio, his eyes coals of fury. "Cursed be your house for bearing this news! You should not have given these lies any thought!"

Galeio lowered his eyes.

"Mokarran," Isurus chided, "it was not his doing."

"And the edict is established?"

Galeio nodded, holding his hands out in appeal to Isurus. "Your brother wasted no time. I only sought to warn you—it was done without my knowledge."

Isurus shook his head, tightening his mouth to steady himself. "I do not hold you responsible, Galeio."

Hattie drew closer and slipped a hand around his arm. "What happens next?" she addressed the others. "What does it mean?"

"It means that to aid Isurus is to align yourself with doom." Mokarran's voice was openly mocking. "I will heed it not at all."

"They know well that fear spreads quicker than fire," Isurus said, almost to himself.

"You would do well to consider what you wish to do now." Aeris spoke for the first time, his face carefully void of emotion.

"I do not need to consider." Isurus pulled himself straighter. His shifting-sea eyes were strangely distant. "You are free to leave me and protect your own houses. I would not bring doom or ill luck—whatever hangs over me—upon any one of you."

He looked to Hattie, and she realized with a start that he was including her with the others.

"Well, it doesn't worry me," she said, with a touch of annoyance. "Everything Altimus says is absolute bosh, and I am not going to give it a second thought."

"Hattie." He spoke almost under his breath, and in a tone that suggested she ought to know better.

His concern only nettled her further. "If I wasn't brought up polite, I'd rip that paper up. Where you go, I go."

Galeio joined her in her protestations of loyalty. "For your father's sake alone, I would follow you to death and destruction. For your own, I pray you give me the honor of remaining at your side."

Isurus's mouth tightened, as if the answer was not what he wanted to hear. "And you mean that? If I am the Doom—"

"Do not dishonor me," said Galeio. "Death is once, dishonor eternal. If doom be ahead, I will meet it with you."

Isurus gave a deep nod and turned to Aeris.

"To break a king's edict as Master of War is a thing worthy of death." The firelight played on his long, angled cheek as he weighed his words. "But I have been loyal to you my whole life. I will not turn from you now."

Isurus looked over at Mokarran, who stood with his arms folded.

Mokarran glared at him until he looked away.

"So be it," said Isurus. "To death or victory."

It was not until dusk the following day that they were able to gain an audience with the Lord of the Shark Kind.

The difference a day made was vast. It reminded Hattie of walking along the docks after a storm, docks that had been neat and trim and swept and were now overturned, twisted, destroyed. She saw the destruction in the faces of the people they passed. Lords who had greeted them and bowed and given gifts—they turned their faces, passed on the other side of the street, or stopped and walked the opposite way.

This destruction of Prionna's had been severe.

Vulpinus left them at the gates, but Mokarran, who had insisted on coming along, followed them all the way. Isurus had argued with him earlier in the afternoon, urging him to consider what it meant to be seen in the streets with a man who was *ana-timeth*, but Mokarran had refused to listen to Isurus since the night before.

Stubborn, Zyaena had said with pride.

On the steps of the great hall, they were met by the shark-keeper with the amber drop in his ear.

"This way," he said, turning and leading them in. From his voice alone, Hattie sensed that this encounter would be colder and more uncomfortable than the last.

The Lord of the Shark Kind stood where they had met him the first time, his arms folded, his old eyes like dead stone.

If his face had been marble before, now it was ice.

"What matter is it that brings you running to my halls like a fish before the fisherman's net?" he demanded in his deep, disinterested voice.

"My brother has set an edict against me, as you have seen. It is unfounded and causes the people great unrest. I merely wish you to put their minds at rest, for the good of Atlantis."

The Lord of the Shark Kind did not move a muscle, save to look over at Mokarran, who stood with his head bowed but his eyes raised.

"What have you to do with me, Mokarran Sphyrna?" he asked.

"May it please your lord," said Mokarran, his insolence only slightly masked, "I come on the same errand as the one who stands before you."

"You do yourself an ill to throw away your house and your reputation thus," said the man, with rebuke in his calm voice.

"May it please your lord, the House of Sphyrna has always had the power to stand where they wish. No matter who opposes them."

Hattie did not think Mokarran had convinced the Lord of the Shark Kind, but he seemed to have scored a point, for the man turned his attention back to Isurus.

"I would entertain his sovereign challenger-king, but I have not the time. I cannot give the people of Atlantis false hope."

"So you believe it, too."

"I believe little that is said by the common man, whether he wear a crown or no. I judge by the earth and the sea and the brother-kind in the waters. They have no reason to lie."

"Then why do you side with my brother?"

"I side with no man," said the Lord of the Shark Kind. "I side with Atlantis. And Atlantis is troubled."

"I wish only the good of Atlantis." For just a moment, Isurus sounded stung.

"To the death, even?"

"If it be required of me, yes. Such I swore when I accepted the crown—which you yourself administered."

"It is not my own memory I doubt, but man's resolve. Your brother also swore such an oath."

"I cannot speak for my brother's resolve, but as you see, I have returned home, through dangers and much toil. I only ask your aid in comforting Atlantis. Surely, if you do not agree with my brother, you can tell the people as much."

"I take counsel neither from you nor from your brother. I will not speak out at this time."

Quiet despair came into Isurus's face. "I am sorry for that. But, of course, you must do what you believe right for Atlantis. As we all must."

"Indeed I shall," said the Lord of the Shark Kind. "And know this: to me, the kingdom is of greater importance than the line of your father, natural or otherwise."

"Can I not appeal to your goodwill?"

"Only the heart of Atlantis brings my goodwill. Unless you know how to open the pillars of the deep, we have nothing more to speak of."

"Then I shall keep your gracious presence no longer."

"The light of the sun be upon you, Isurus Lamnidae," answered the Lord of the Shark Kind. And for the briefest moment, Hattie thought she saw regret in his face.

They were silent until the steps and the wide flagstones before the hall were behind them. Vulpinus fell in behind them when they reached the gate, following at a distance.

"So." Isurus let his breath out quietly.

"You must not lose heart." Mokarran's voice was taut, his eyes kindling. "The Lord of the Shark Kind is a fool. It is clear that he is on your brother's side."

"It is not clear." Isurus looked at his friend with reproach. "He has every right to stand for the protection of Atlantis. Were I a threat, I should hope he would not falter in removing me."

"You are not a threat, and he knows it well!"

Isurus looked at Mokarran as if he meant to speak, but thought better of it. Hattie slipped her hand into his, and they walked the rest of the way in silence.

It was dark by the time they reached the house of Sphyrna. The courtyard was empty, save for a table lamp set near the fountain and a lone figure reading by its light.

"I wondered where you were," said Taurus, looking up from his book. The light of the flame played on his hollowed cheeks.

"We were with the Shark Kind."

"Is that why Mokarran is in such a state?" Taurus's glance went to the man's retreating back.

"That and the proclamation. Did you read it?"

"Alas, yes."

Isurus gave a deep sigh. "Taurus, have you given thought to what it means to remain in my company, now that the cloud of doom lies over me?" The heaviness of his voice weighed on Hattie like a stone.

"Only Prionna said that. You recall I put a scorpion in her hair last time she told me I was destined for a bad death."

A flicker of a smile passed over Isurus's sad face. "The Lord of the Shark Kind said it as well."

Taurus spit on the floor. "Poisonous woman. What had she to do with the Lord of the Shark Kind?"

"Nothing. But he has spoken. I am under doom, and perhaps even the Doom of Atlantis. To aid me is forbidden."

Taurus gave a savage laugh. "Let them try to rip my fingers from your aid. We are kin!"

Isurus's voice gentled. Hattie had heard him sound just so whenever he spoke to children in Roke Point. "Taurus, sometimes you are unwise and do that which is not in your own interest."

"There is more to it than wisdom. There is—honor to consider, and—" He cast about for words.

"Go, Taurus." Isurus's voice was quiet. "Think no more on it."

"But I do not wish to," said Taurus, growing firmer.

"But fate—"

"I don't care about fate! Who do you think I am?"

"You have already suffered more on my account than you ought."

"There is no decision to be made, Isurus. I am with you."

"Will you not come to regret that?"

Taurus looked up at him, incredulous. "I have thought on it for a day and yet a little more. What else do you require of me?"

"I would not have your blood on my hands. You know what has been said about your death, and if—"

"By the Brotherhood, do you really believe that? How loud must I shout before you listen to what I say, not what you want to hear?"

Taurus's voice echoed off the courtyard, followed by dead silence. Hattie hardly dared breathe.

Then Taurus's mouth twisted. "Is it that you do not want me?" His gaunt face was hurt now, the anger melted away entirely by this new thought.

Isurus let out a long, shuddering breath. "Of course not."

"Then let my fate be on my own head. And let me stand at your side, where I should be."

Taurus went to a low table against the wall and poured a swallow of wine into two glasses. "Here, cousin."

Isurus accepted the offered wine silently. He lifted it to his lips but could not seem to bring himself to taste it.

The firelight played off of Taurus's grim face as he raised his own glass. "To death or victory," he said, and drank it to the dregs.

FIFTEEN

The Traitor's Game

He was gone.

It was dark yet, but the faint sound of birds hinted at the coming of dawn. Hattie rolled over, a whisper of nausea unsettling her. She would need to eat, soon.

She sat up, reaching for her outer wrap. The mornings were cool without the sun.

She found him alone on the marble steps, staring out at the water that reflected the paling sky, and she put her arms around him. He shifted and relaxed at her touch.

He reached around and held her hand. She could tell by his touch that he was tired. "Don't tell me you've been up all night."

"It doesn't matter." He sighed, his voice low.

"It matters to me."

He gave the briefest edge of a laugh, low in his throat.

"Are you well?" he asked. "It has been a long and terrible few days."

"Of course I am. It takes a lot more than some ancient superstition to worry me." She ran her fingers over his glowing tattoo where it stretched down into his forearm. "And you?"

"What if it is true?"

"That wasn't my question," chided Hattie gently.

"But if I am the Doom—my love, how could I look you in the eye? I married you and brought you here, and if I am—"

"Isurus." She turned him to face her. "Nothing would change. I don't believe in dooms and fates, and even if I did, it wouldn't change anything."

"What if I change?" His face was conflicted. Afraid to ask, needing to know.

"Are you going to?" She caught his gaze and held it.

"These things are more powerful than you think, dearest."

"I told you, I do not believe them."

"But when everyone else does?"

"I will stick by you." She smiled and kissed him gently. "Let's leave this be. It doesn't bother me, so don't allow it to stand between us."

Something in his face gave way and he nodded, relenting.

"Now, my dear, you are exhausted. Rest, and if you can't, go swim. Shake these thoughts. Your brother is not going to win this easily."

He lifted her hand and kissed it gratefully.

Mokarran appeared with the sun, wearing brilliant white and blue which set off his dark hair and eyes like a Greek hero in a book. Beneath his arm, he carried a thick parchment.

"Isurus, I have been studying the histories for wisdom, and I have found something that may be of use to us."

"Speak, then," said Isurus. He had taken a swim and changed into fresh clothes, and it seemed to have revived him. Now the servants were bringing out grapes and bread and honey-wine and dates to a great golden table on a pavilion beside the water.

For Hattie, they couldn't have come soon enough.

"It is a traitor's game, employed by Trophimus in the last age, when his sister stole the throne from him and had him locked away for madness."

"Overthrow the king, then?"

"It is quicker and less bloody than a war, you know that. If we fail, we die, but the people are not touched. Not so with war."

"A coup." Hattie put a grape in her mouth and fought the urge to close her eyes as her head swam and her stomach protested.

"Yes." Isurus pressed his knuckles against his chin as he thought.

"It is not expressly barred by law, not by word or statute."

"Have you thought how we would bring it about? All will fear to turn, now."

"I have thought." Mokarran leaned forward eagerly. His tunic slipped on his shoulder a little, and Hattie saw the edge of the black ink that adorned his back and shoulders. She remembered the glint in his eye when he had explained to her that the stingray was a warning to his enemies.

"In the full turn of the moon and half a turn more, Altimus will hold the Festival of the Sun Throne. It is customary that the finest four-hundred of the soldiers come to the king in his throne room and perform their feats, so that he may see the strength of his army. As Master of War, Aeris will be in charge of choosing the men. Once in the throne room, we can overpower the king and force him to abdicate."

Isurus shook his head doubtfully. "If you think my brother will concede that easily—"

But Mokarran raised his hand. "That is only the beginning. Zyaena is nearly every day in Prionna's company—and better still, in her chambers while Prionna is gone. We will play their game. We will find writings that make it plain that you cannot be the Doom. Furthermore, we will find writings that speak against the outrages of Altimus."

"You cannot manipulate prophecies and ancient writings, Mokarran."

"Not in truth. But that is what Prionna does. And if we do not find a way to make you pleasing in the people's sight, she will have won. This way, we will have the people, and we will have the throne. Your people may be afraid, but they need you, Isurus."

Watching Mokarran's dark eyes burn, Hattie felt real hope, for the first time in days.

Isurus remained deep in thought. "And what of the Lord of the Shark Kind?"

A muscle twitched in Mokarran's jaw at the mention of the man. "If we commit no bloodshed, he cannot be against us. He has said he will take no sides in this matter."

"I wish I could believe him. His will changes with every tide."

Mokarran's voice held a bitter note. "Then it will soon be due to turn back to you and away from your brother. Take heart."

"Is there no way to change his mind?" asked Hattie.

Mokarran set the parchment aside and took a piece of bread, tearing it in half. "If we could control the throes of the earth, that would convince him."

"But if we shed no blood, he will have no cause to be against us. It will have to be enough." Isurus bit into a date and washed it down with the watered wine. "It will be as the *ith-ili*. If we win the board on the traitor's move, there is no transgression. But if we lose…."

Mokarran's eyes held a dangerous glint. "Oh, Isurus. We will not lose."

Zyaena leaned her hands on the table, moving her finger slowly down the page. The breeze blew her hair over the book and into her face. Absently, she reached up and moved it out of the way. She seemed the only one in the room who was perfectly calm, as if everything did not hang on this moment.

Galeio sat by with parchment and quill, ready to make note of what she read. Isurus and Hattie were together on the low couch, and Mokarran leaned against the back, one elbow on his upraised knee.

Zyaena turned the page; the soft swish of the paper seemed to fill the room. "Here." She looked up at them and read from where her finger held the place.

"*The words of Nalak, in the third year of the season of growing, to those who come after. And at this time, I looked over the sea, and behold! it was clear to me that the hearts of men are yet as they were from the beginning, running to trouble and sorrow as the rivers run to the seas.*"

Mokarran cleared his throat meaningfully.

Zyaena glanced up at him with a touch of warning in her eyes and continued in a quiet, clear voice: "*And there will again come a time when the pride of our ancestors is nearly forgotten, and strife will arise, yea, even between brothers, because of the pride that is in the heart of man. And brother will covet brother's place—*

"She has marked the lines about brothers," said Zyaena.

Galeio wrote swiftly, glancing over her shoulder at the page.

Mokarran cast a contemptuous hand toward the book. "Brother will covet brother's place? Does she intend to condemn you with that? It is as fine a description of Altimus as ever I heard!"

"Peace, Mokarran. We have far to go." Isurus rubbed his neck wearily.

Zyaena continued:

In the season of the running of the blued fish,

under the stars of Achilles,

portents will come and after memory's holding

the Doom will be revealed.

And this will be the sign you shall seek:

In one day the king shall lose every hound,

Fate seek the stranger.

Doom comes upon the mighty, but in humility

are the mighty saved.

"We still have the hounds." Mokarran folded his arms. "And unless Prionna plans to destroy the runs under the watchful eyes of the Shark Kind, they are not like to disappear. The sharks may be thinning and the blued fish returning, yet Prionna does not rule the stars."

Zyaena read on:

Watch, ye sons of the sea; your doom is at hand.

With soundless storm rises

the fate of Atlantis.

With sea's rising and stone's breaking

and throes of the earth

it comes.

Woe, woe to the proud and those raised high

for swift fell Icarus.

But—

From the west, the sun will rise

In his hand he will bring hope

In his line the blood of foreigners will run,

the sea establish his reign.

The hunters will perish, the hound judge,

might be spun in woman's hand.

As the First Atlantean rose to save all,

so the Last Atlantean will be the saving of his people

and world's ending,

with sweet to salt

will end.

The bane of the Doom is the Fate

and woe to the Doom.

Galeio leaned over the page beside Zyaena and pointed to a passage. "There, we can use that."

Isurus leaned over to see. "The sea, establish my reign?"

"If we win the coup, it may be said that the sea has returned you blameless." Galeio leaned back. "The people need comfort, not the fulfillment of prophecy. They simply wish to be reassured that doom is not coming upon them."

"But what if it is?" Isurus took a step back. "If doom were coming, would it not be better that they know and are prepared?"

"Isurus." Galeio's face was grave. "If doom is coming, the people are much safer in your hands."

"In his line the blood of foreigners will run." Zyaena ran her finger over the line, then glanced at Hattie. "Prionna believes it speaks of the Carmians, but your line will have foreign blood too, Isurus.

When a child comes...."

"It would be a fine thing to point to, but it is well that there is no child yet," Isurus said solemnly. "This is not the time to be vulnerable." He glanced at Hattie with an innocent smile.

A shock ran through her, breaking her into a sweat; the smile she gave him was forced. If only he knew.

"I have had my fill of this accursed prophecy." Mokarran shifted in restless scorn, impatient with the task, though it had been his idea to search the book in the first place.

Hattie raised her face to the gray sky and smelled the familiar fresh dampness of a coming squall. "It looks like rain." The wind, too, was quickening.

"I nearly have it." Galeio looked from his parchment to the book and made one last notation. "Thank you, Zyaena, for this service."

Zyaena shut the heavy book, glancing at the sky. "I must return it before someone notices it is gone."

"Take every caution," Mokarran warned, unfolding his arms.

"Prionna is in the hills today, fulfilling some duty to Sol in a far village. She will not be back until nightfall. But the book must not get wet, and I must avoid her servants."

"Take one of the household guard." Mokarran jerked his head to the doorway.

"I will be faster alone." Zyaena straightened, holding the book to her chest as a servant put her cloak upon her shoulders. "For Atlantis."

"Wait," she had said. "Let them destroy themselves."

Waiting was all he had done.

Wait to accuse the proud, undeserving king. Wait to mourn the brother he hated. Wait to destroy the ones who openly accused him of treachery. Wait to strike the proud, smug look from that ash-streaked face.

She loved waiting; she took deepest pleasure from building her plans to their greatest height before revealing them. As for him, give him a spear and let him do what he might, swift and clean.

This time, she was right. Victory would be sweeter for the waiting. But how he longed for that day.

How he wanted to see him fall.

SIXTEEN

I Wish We Could Have Been Cowards

It happened seven days before they were to make their move.

It was evening, the light of day mere paleness on the western horizon, and Zyaena returned for the night hours later than expected.

Hattie met her in the hall as she threw back her hood and unclasped her cloak. It was a warm day—whatever she had been doing, she hadn't wanted to be seen.

"Hattie! Where is Isurus? Or Mokarran? I have terrible news."

"I am here." Isurus emerged from the adjoining room. "Your brother went out a couple hours ago to inspect the goods coming in. Tryaena went with him, just in case."

He waited patiently for Zyaena to catch her breath, so quiet and still that Hattie knew he was afraid.

"Today, she bade me go my way at the normal time, when her public business was concluded, and as I left, I realized I had left out a certain book she wanted put away, and I did not want there to be any cause for her to find fault, so I returned."

Zyaena took a breath as if to calm herself, though her exterior seemed already to be made of iron. "They intercepted a half-burned note. Nothing they could understand—I heard them read it—but they suspect you, Isurus, or a member of this household."

"Whose was it?"

"I do not know. Possibly a missive between Galeio and Aeris, as they are most often in the palace, but it does not matter. They will come looking here. I do not know how soon."

"And if they come, they will find enough to overturn our plans."

Isurus twisted his fist in his hand.

"I fear if Mokarran is out, they may take him for questioning before he can return here or know what has happened."

Isurus set his hand on Zyaena's arm. "I have brought this trouble upon your house. I will find him and warn him, and then I will leave until the danger has passed."

Zyaena shook her head. "We looked for this, and we would do it again. Mokarran would say the same if he was here. You know that."

"Nonetheless, I will seek him. Vulpinus!"

The tall guard appeared from the shadows, his fist pressed to his shoulder. "My lord?"

"Come, we must away to the wharf." Isurus kissed Hattie softly on the cheek. "Admit no one until I return."

The two departed, leaving the young women in a too-silent, too-empty hall.

In the daytime, the massive structures of Atlantis were impressive and warm. At night, they seemed hollow and dangerous.

Zyaena sat on a low couch, examining the embroidered wrist of her dress, and Hattie knew she was afraid. She had seen the same look in the women of Roke Point when a nor'easter was brewing.

"Isurus will find him," she said.

Zyaena nodded mutely.

A fist pounded upon the great door, followed by the hard rattle of the gate. Zyaena started up.

"It could be one of our men," offered Hattie.

Zyaena drew in a deep breath. "Mokarran does not pound on his own door so. And if it is Isurus, then there is trouble."

Hattie knew that well enough.

A servant met them, coming from the doors. "It is Stellarus, the captain of the king's guard. He wishes admittance and to speak to the challenger-king."

Hattie drew herself up. "I will hear him in my husband's stead."

"Wait—I will speak to him. Stay here." Zyaena held up one of her hands as if to protect Hattie. "I am the woman of the house. He will answer to me for this disturbance."

Hattie followed her to the door, staying out of sight.

The torchlight outside the door lit upon the man's large nose, lost itself in his curly dark hair.

"I said I wished to speak to the challenger-king." His voice was cold.

"He cannot be troubled with meeting you," answered Zyaena. "But as lady of this house, I demand that you cease this disturbance and heel to your master."

He lifted his lip in a sneer. "I come to say that the days of your power are coming to an end. Tell your brother that the king will have the traitor from his halls yet."

"I do not carry messages for men like you." Zyaena gave a nod to her doorkeeper and stood like iron, watching Stellarus until the doors closed between them.

She let her breath out and turned to Hattie, her face aflame with an expression remarkably like Mokarran. "There are few people I truly despise, and he is one of them."

"I have been warned against him, but I do not see him much."

"He is a cold-blooded man and a killer. It was he who arranged to have Crestus killed. If I could have spat in his face just now, I would have."

"I'm surprised you didn't," Hattie said softly. She didn't know if she would have had the self-control.

Zyaena sat down and put her head in her hands.

"You should sleep," Hattie murmured. "I am sure they will be all right."

"I do not know if I can." Her voice was tired.

Hattie sat down next to her and put her arm around her shoulders. Zyaena gave a long sigh and laid her head against Hattie's. "Hattie, after I lost Crestus, the idea of losing Mokarran became too much to bear. Even if he is all right, the waiting is awful."

Hattie reached behind Zyaena, stroking her long hair, separating it into strands. "Where I grew up, the sea is our livelihood as well. It is a cold sea, deep and wild, and storms blow up out of nowhere. We have lost many of our men to the sea. On stormy nights, we must wait."

"And how do you pass the time?"

"Well," said Hattie, beginning to braid the strands together, "when my brothers still lived at home, sometimes I would put on the kettle and bake, or knit a new scarf. 'When it is finished, they will be home,' I would say to myself, and think about how I'd laugh at my fear in the morning."

"Did you ever lose anyone?"

It took Hattie a moment to gather her strength before answering. "Yes. My brother Jack. He was four years older than me. He had a beautiful wife…and twins, a boy and a girl."

"How old are they?"

"About a year old, now. But when we lost him, they were barely two months. I think about them every day."

"Does it ever lessen? The pain?"

A wave of sorrow washed over Hattie. "You don't ever lose it. But it does get better."

"I hold it back for the sake of my brother, but at night, when there is nothing but quiet and darkness…I fear sleep now. I am so tired of the pain."

"All sorrows pass," Hattie said gently, remembering Isurus's words to her on the heights above the coast.

Tears hung on Zyaena's long lashes. "I knew Crestus all my life." She gave a little smile. "He was so kind, and he laughed. He laughed more than anyone I know. Some days, I still cannot bring myself to believe he is really gone."

Hattie tied off the braid with the ribbon from her own hair. "What was he like?"

"He was strong. And he was good. He could swim like a shark."

"Isurus tells me about him sometimes. He says he was the mightiest hunter among them."

"And he was. I think Altimus was jealous, for Crestus was the only one taller than he. He was swifter, too, and perhaps stronger, if he had tried. They never made trial of it between them."

The ache in Hattie's chest grew heavier. "It seems Altimus is jealous of many. I do not understand why."

Zyaena gave a small shake of her head. "Some men are born with the need to prove themselves. It does not seem to matter whether you are a fisherman's son or a king's son."

Hattie nodded. She had seen it, too.

"Crestus came to me one evening and said he'd had an audience with Altimus. He said they only spoke of old prophecies and their meanings, but I knew, deep down, that there was more than he was telling me. He was ever a good friend to Isurus. Everyone knew it. The next week, he was dead."

"He was very brave." Hattie knew how little comfort such words brought, but she had to say them all the same.

Zyaena's jaw clenched. "He was. And I supported him. One cannot live without honor." She let out a slow breath. "But—sometimes I wish we could have been cowards so that we could be here together. Just at times…when the sea is clear and there is a hunt in the air, or when there is rain and the birds wheel among it, or when the stars are so bright that they rival the moon."

"Sometimes I think that, when I remember life in Maine. If Isurus had stayed there with me, there would be none of this danger, none of this waiting and not knowing."

Zyaena's eyes were large and deep and sorrowful. "I think of these people, my brother, your husband, Aeris, Crestus, all the people I grew up with and love—and then I think—if this goes wrong, we'll be wiped from history, not just our deeds, but our golden times, our laughter and the love we have for each other. And I wonder—if our choices will have been worth it. If it would have been better, in the end, to be cowards."

"But our choices are made. And they cannot be undone."

"For the better, I suppose. Otherwise, in our weak times we would run back to undo what we wish could be undone."

She leaned her head against Hattie's shoulder.

"I know. Some nights I dream about being on the wharf the moment my brother Jack got on that boat, going out into that storm. There was a floundering boat, and he was going to rescue the sailors. Sometimes I try to talk him out of it, or I have a reason he needs to come with me, and I change his mind. But he knew what he was doing. He understood the danger, and he did it anyway. Just as Crestus did, and as your brother does."

Zyaena's next words were almost a whisper. "I am glad that Tryaena went with him. Few people cross Tryaena."

"Prionna said something about Tryaena when I first came…something about her stabbing me for Isurus. I assume it is bosh, but—"

"Oh, that. It is right that you should not listen to Prionna, but it is also true that Tryaena loved Isurus from childhood. Her father was the king's most trusted bodyguard—her family was given a lord's house generations ago, for service rendered to the king, and they've been the best fighting house since." Zyaena gave a tired sigh. "If Isurus had wanted to marry, true, he could have chosen her. He was adamantly against marriage before…. But she is a good fighter, and loves no one else. All she has left is to defend him with her life."

Hattie sat quietly for a minute with the revelation. "She must have been angry with Altimus," she said at last.

"It was likely Prionna's spite for her that made her mention her to you. Tryaena refused to attend the coronation, and as head of her house, paid Altimus a great slight."

"And he did nothing?"

"You don't kill a Carcharhinus outright. Not unless they let you." Zyaena smiled as if it was a jest. "But you can see why she hates Vulpinus so."

"I suppose so."

A heartbeat of silence passed. Then, across the room, the door swung open.

Mokarran entered, followed by Isurus and his guard. They appeared unharmed, their garments as clean as when they had left.

"Tryaena has gone her way for the night." Isurus came over, taking Hattie's hands and kissing her in greeting. "The reckoning has not yet come."

Mokarran caught his eye, and something grim and dangerous passed between them. "We will double the watch, to be safe," Mokarran said, unclasping his cloak and draping it over his arm.

Isurus mustered a smile for Hattie. "Let us get a little sleep while we can. Tomorrow will come swift enough."

SEVENTEEN

For the Good of Atlantis

"Nearly a month and a half of waiting, and now this." Mokarran drummed his ringed fingers upon the table. "Less than a week before the coup."

"We cannot afford to risk it now," Isurus said, his gaze meeting each face gathered around him—Hattie, Galeio, Mokarran and Zyaena, Aeris, Taurus, Tryaena. "Let us wait, if we must. Destroy what we have and avoid detection. I can bear the wait, but I could not bear your needless deaths."

"Perhaps they are needed." Taurus shrugged—a strangely easy gesture, considering his words. "Altimus will be on his guard until he thinks he has found the rogue piece on the board."

"He knows well enough that I do not bide here merely to postpone my death."

Tryaena set her hands on the table. "Send the guard. Put him under oath to say it was he trying to spread rebellion. Take care of the two greatest dangers at once." She sent a dagger's glare toward Vulpinus, who stood silently beyond the table.

Vulpinus raised his eyebrows in surprise and drew back ever so slightly.

Hattie had once seen a rat terrier going after a hound twice its size; the hound had stood its ground, but had drawn its head upward with every new strike until finally the terrier could no longer reach it.

So it seemed with those two.

"If my lord wishes it," Vulpinus spoke gravely, "I will do it."

Isurus looked at him as though he were mad. "Not on my life.

Tryaena, please. No more of this."

Galeio cleared his throat. He had stood to one side the whole time, silent, his hands folded. Now he spoke. "I wish to remind those gathered here that drastic decisions are rarely the best course. I have been in Altimus's counsel, even this morning, and while he wishes to destroy us—you most of all, sovereignty—he has no plans of substance yet. We must keep him from discovering the truth, but we have, perhaps, some time. Days, not hours, to come to a decision."

"What is your counsel?" The restlessness in Isurus's eyes lessened ever so slightly; he was relieved, Hattie thought, to be guided by Galeio.

"Do nothing for a day's time. Let the preparations for the coup rest. Keep your own counsel. After which time, we will see what may come."

"The fisherman who waits to see the fish before casting his net returns home with empty hands." Mokarran's voice held warning.

"True enough." Galeio gave a patient nod. "But if Altimus catches us too soon, we will be in the shark's mouth before there is a chance to save Atlantis from his rule. And that we cannot risk."

Night came on with a profusion of stars. Galeio alone had remained after the others had gone their way, and Hattie sensed something unusual in his manner. The smoothness he usually wore, plain as his tunic, was laid aside for the night.

"Are you well, sovereign?" he asked.

Isurus sank onto a low seat, the exhaustion of the last few days settling in the lines of his shoulders. "I am well enough. Do not worry for me. My shoulders are stronger than they look." He glanced up, accompanying his words with a wry smile.

"I wish to tell you what I did not want to say in company."

Isurus motioned for him to speak, but Hattie could see plain as day that he wished he did not have to hear it.

"I did not wish to bring this fear needlessly before the others, but I believe Taurus is right. Altimus will need a scapegoat. I have watched him more closely than any in the last year, and I can tell you, the coup is in great danger while he holds open suspicion."

Isurus glanced at Hattie as if wishing she was not privy to this conversation, but he said nothing to her. "Is there no other way to appease him?"

Galeio shook his head.

Isurus closed his eyes for the space of three heartbeats. "I will go to my brother, then. With my death, all suspicion will be gone. And with your wisdom, Taurus will reign well enough after a coup."

"Sovereignty." There was quiet reproach in his voice. "That is not what I meant."

"I will not allow you to do it, Galeio." Isurus pushed his hair back and looked away, refusing to give it consideration.

"Who better? Name me a man you need less."

"I will not! Man is not made to rule over life and death. I will not do it. I cannot have your blood on my hands."

"My blood will not be on your hands, sovereignty." His voice was gentle, like a father to his son. "You must never think that."

"Had I stayed away—"

"You know you could not have. By the blood in your veins and the mark on your arm, you could not."

"But neither can I have your death. I—could not bear it if you were killed."

A grim smile pulled at the corner of Galeio's mouth. "I swore I would follow you, even to the *ta-ilith*. I will not tread the coward's path."

Isurus's voice was hard, on the edge of breaking. "You will not. I command it."

"Isurus, Atlantis is deeply perplexed. They fear Altimus, they fear you. The sooner you can provide them the steadfastness they need, the better it will be for all."

"Without you, victory would have no savor."

"Some victories never will. We must act for the good of Atlantis, not for ourselves."

Isurus drew a breath as if it pained him. "Promise me that you will not do anything foolhardy."

"Nothing foolhardy." Galeio's face was gentle.

After a silence, he reached inside his tunic and pulled out a parchment. "I thought I might bring to your attention a line I found in the Book of the Blessed, before I go."

He spread it out upon the table and the two of them bent over it.

Hattie watched them quietly. She had not been feeling well of late, and she had not the energy to get up and look over their shoulders, but she could see some of the weight lift from Isurus as his eyes followed Galeio's finger over the words, as a child with his tutor.

At last they both straightened. Isurus's face was weary. "So, it is well? There is nothing further to be discussed tonight?"

Galeio rolled the parchment up, and there was a finality in his motions that moved Hattie. "It is well, my sovereign. It is well."

"I shall see you in the morning, then."

"In the dawn," Galeio promised. He thrust the parchment back into his tunic.

Hattie walked him to the door and held it open for him, and he gave her a reassuring nod. "My lady, goodnight."

"And to you, my lord," she said. "A good night."

In the short time it had taken her to escort Galeio to the door, Isurus had fallen asleep in his chair. Often sleep smoothed away the worries in his face, but not so tonight. His head was upon his shoulder, his brows still knit, his jaw clenched as if something hurt.

She wanted to take it away, all this pain and sorrow, all the fear of sudden death and loss of everything that made life sweet. And she couldn't. Watching him, it was almost unbearable.

She leaned down and moved the hair off his forehead, kissing it.

"Oh, Hattie, what is it?" His eyes snapped open, the color of the restless sea.

"You fell asleep in your chair."

"I must be more tired than I thought."

"You should go to bed. You will kill yourself of exhaustion long before Altimus gets the chance."

He forced a smile, and she saw admission in his eyes. "Very well, I shall go to bed. Are you coming too?"

"In a bit. I think I shall go and walk under the stars."

He caught her hand briefly and kissed it. "Take care—I will leave Vulpinus up to keep a watch."

"I'll keep to the water and the garden. I can hear anyone coming."

"So be it." Isurus remained long enough to charge Vulpinus with her safety, then left her.

The night was still. The stars, bright and strong, shone like distant suns. It was a comfort, more than she could have guessed when she was leaving Maine, to have the same stars she'd known from childhood in this sky, like old friends. For a short time, she could forget the hard, cruel world around her and remember that in Roke Point they would be chopping wood for winter, the boats brewing hot coffee for the deckhands, the women planning quilting bees and corn huskings.

It was good to know that home, even without her, even though she no longer belonged to it, was well and happy.

Footsteps echoed quietly in the corridor on the other side of the pillars. She ducked out of sight.

It was Galeio, walking slowly as if deep in thought, his face a little sad.

He had not seen her. He paused at a stone rail and leaned his arms on it, looking at the night sky. A long while he stood gazing up at the stars, and then he pulled his chain off his neck and regarded the hammered medallion on the end of it.

"And so farewell, and so farewell. To the golden city shall we go, and in the dawn meet one another again. And so farewell." His voice murmured the words gently, as if he had drawn them up from the deepest seas to cherish close to his heart.

She came around the pillar, and he looked up swiftly. "My queen." He swallowed rapidly and gave her a deep nod. "You are out late."

"As are you. You bid Isurus a good night quite some time ago."

"Yes. Yes, I suppose I did." He clasped his hands behind his back. "We had finished what needed to be discussed, however, and that was the end of it."

It was quiet between them.

"I did not mean to intrude," said Hattie. "I was simply looking at the stars, and—"

"No, you are right. You have intruded on my thoughts no less than

I have intruded on yours, and I will take my leave now if you wish."

"I cannot believe my thoughts could possibly be more important than yours right now."

He smiled, but it seemed to her sad and a little unsteady. "On the contrary." He spread out his fingers and lay his hand against the cool marble. "I think you have a greater power to give him victory than any of the rest of us. You must not forget that."

Hattie's heart twisted inside her.

Galeio's piercing blue eyes met hers, and they were earnest. "Swear to me you will remember? Love him when all hope seems lost. Stand by him. And he may find strength in being a king for you when even Atlantis cannot inspire it in him."

Hattie nodded and looked out at the quiet water lapping below the stone. "Are you sure?"

"Very sure. In your hand lies more power to help or harm him than any one of ours. And he needs it."

"Then I will."

"I thank you." He put his hand to his chest. "Our world hangs on it. I wish I could have done more to lift that burden."

"But you have, and you will—"

"No." Galeio cut her off gently. "No longer."

"Galeio, you aren't—"

"I will go to Altimus tonight. It was my note he discovered, and I can explain away all else, leaving the others safe. I trust my own tongue and my strength not to waver."

"What will Isurus say?"

"I have never betrayed him before—this I regret I must do as a last service. But he will see the sense in keeping his mouth closed, for the good of the kingdom."

"Is there—is there nothing I can do?"

"I swore to follow him even to the *ta-ilith,* and vows mean nothing if they are not kept when tested. I have made my decision. It is well." He set his hand on top of hers reassuringly. "You are a fine woman, Hattie. It was more than fate when Isurus washed up on your shore. Perhaps he needed to lose the throne for a time, if for no other reason than to find you."

He glanced down at the water and pushed himself away from the rail with reluctant hands.

"Well, I must go."

"I will walk with you." Hattie fell in step beside him.

They were silent, the only sound their soft footsteps and the lapping of the water. When they reached the end of the hall, where the pavement turned into the footpaths that wound through the gardens, Hattie paused. "Would you like me to go now?"

"Stay a bit longer." He gave a little smile. "You give me courage."

"I will stay as long as you wish it."

He tilted his head far back and breathed deeply of the cool air. "It is a fine night."

"Very fine. Where I come from, it is getting ready to turn cold now."

"I suppose you miss it."

"Sometimes. But I belong with Isurus."

"And he with you." He glanced down at his hands. "Be good to him. You may understand more than most, I know, but I had the privilege of teaching him many things. He is like an island rising from the sea. You only ever see the surface, and there is a world more that he hides from all but a few. He is burdened, and the burden will only grow greater. Help him keep his head above the sea."

Hattie sought his eyes and looked straight into them. "I promise. I will."

Galeio gave a breath of a laugh. "Then I bid you goodnight and farewell." He lifted her hand and kissed it.

"Goodnight," she whispered as he turned and trudged alone down the garden path. "And God be with you."

"I gave you the world."

The morning sun played in her hair like strands of gold.

"And I gave you power," he said. "When I ascended, I gave you everything you wished."

"You never asked what I wished." Her voice could be like iron when she wanted. "And I want this."

"It will only bring you sorrow and grief."

"Then I will take the sorrow and grief," she said, and there were tears in her eyes. He almost could have relented, seeing those steel-blue eyes, gazing out at him from their deep wells.

"No." He turned away from her and looked instead at the city, bathed in brilliant gold.

EIGHTEEN

In the Dawn We Shall Meet

As it happens sometimes, when a great change comes, the morning began with forgetting.

Hattie woke feeling less sick than most recent mornings, and her first thought was gratefulness.

Then a smash of glass broke the silence, and everything from the night before came to her in a rush. She ran out into the hall even as shards of glass from a broken wine-jar slid across the floor, a couple falling soundlessly into the water.

Isurus was standing bent over a chair, his hands gripping the back of it, his face twisted as if in pain.

"What is it?"

She came up behind him. On the floor, ruined by the spilled wine, was a note, swiftly written. Zyaena's hand.

"What happened?"

"Galeio has been charged as a traitor."

"And?" Her heart seemed to stop as she waited for his reply.

"They will hold the *ta-ilith* this afternoon." His hands dug into the back of the chair. He stared at the glass on the floor, unseeing.

"And there is nothing we can do?"

"Nothing." He clenched his fists. "I should have forced him to leave. I should have—I should have stopped him."

She went to him, came up beside him, ignoring the grind of the glass under her sandals. "He chose, Isurus."

He shook his head adamantly, turning his head away from her. Gently she reached out, rubbing his shoulder. "I spoke with him, last

205

night. He chose."

Isurus buried his face in her shoulder and began to sob, hot tears soaking through the linen. It frightened her—she had seen him cry before, with tears standing in his eyes, but not like this.

"He knew what he was doing," she said softly, rubbing his back, trying to give him some comfort. "He said that it had to be done, if your cause was to continue."

"If that be so, I wish there was no cause to help."

"Oh, my love." She pressed her lips against his forehead.

"Atlantis itself rises against this outrage. Any one of us might have died the *ta-ilith*, but him—?"

"Can—can anything be done?"

"I think not." His voice was hoarse. "I would take his place if I could."

There was a knock, and Vulpinus ushered in a servant of the palace. "My lady Prionna wishes admittance," the man said, bowing.

"The lady Prionna is here?" Isurus took a step toward the man as if he had not heard him correctly.

"She wishes to speak with you and seeks your promise that there will be no treachery."

Isurus belted on his knife. "There will be none from me."

"That is enough for my lady."

Isurus and Hattie met her near the door.

She was alone; her guard remained outside. Her eyes lingered for a long, hard moment on Hattie's face. Hattie returned the look steadily until the woman shifted her gaze to Isurus.

"I lay the condemnation at your feet." Her quiet voice seemed loud in the empty room.

Isurus shifted his feet, said nothing. His eyes remained on her face in quiet reproach.

Prionna lifted her chin, her jaw like a vice. "Contrary to what you may believe, I cared very much about Galeio. He was my father's greatest friend, and I admired him. His betrayal, to me, was worse than death." Her voice lowered to a near whisper. "I hate you, for you turned his heart against me."

"I never turned it," said Isurus. "He never changed."

An angry spasm crossed her stoic face. Hattie could see that the truth struck home.

"You do not know that. Where were you, that year you were gone? What cause had you to stay away so long if you care about Atlantis as you say you do?"

"You know very well why I was delayed." His voice was soft, controlled.

"Altimus can be both hasty and harsh, I grant it. But Atlantis's honor would be affronted if its best son were to die in the worst way." Her voice turned hard and flat and her words quickened, as if she only had the strength to say the words once. "Galeio Triakidae had admirers on both sides. He was offered oleander, and he accepted. I thought that you should know." Reluctantly, Prionna drew something out of a cloth and set it into Isurus's hand.

"So, then. It is done." His fingers closed reverently over Galeio's medal.

"And his body will be thrown outside the city in the wild places, at the king's command."

Isurus looked up, his voice hard, on the edge of unsteadiness.

"Was not murdering him enough? Must you flaunt the ancient laws by refusing the honor due all men?"

"He was a traitor." She almost broke there. It was as if she did not quite believe what she was saying.

"He was loyal to the son of his king! Let him be buried with his fathers."

Prionna's eyes were like ice. "No. Any rites or ceremonies will be met with severe punishments. He will not be honored or mourned."

When Isurus spoke again, his voice was oddly gentle. "Who decrees this? You, or my brother?"

"Your brother's words are my own, and my very heart is as his own. I say again—" a spasm crossed her face— "he will not be mourned. Let it be known that no man crosses the Shark King."

"And true it is," whispered Isurus, his eyes like flint. "There was no man better than he in all Atlantis. You know that. His blood cries out for justice."

She swallowed hard. "It was you who brought about his death. You, coming back with—" Her gaze flashed like a knife to Hattie. Her meaning was clear enough. "It is because of your coming that he died."

Isurus took a step toward her.

"Stay back." Her hand went to the knife at her side.

"Fear nothing. I would not touch you. But know this—his blood is on your hands. You, whose life he preserved, whose father he loved."

Everything left her face in a rush of still, pale anger.

"I will see the end of you, Isurus Lamnidae. I will be there at your end, and you will see that it was a mistake to cross me."

She backed up with a mocking bow and left, a terrible smile on her face.

Isurus blew into the garden like a squall over the rocks of Roke Point, his face set like stone, Hattie following quietly.

They found Taurus pacing alongside the water.

"It is done," Isurus said. "But it was poison, not the sharks."

"I heard. Aeris came. He told me." Taurus's voice was hollow. His hands were clenched in fists.

Hattie stood in the shade and watched them, let her heartbeat slow. Prionna's face, white and mocking, was burned into her memory. She was sorry for Galeio, afraid for Isurus.

Isurus went to his cousin and laid his arm over his shoulders. "He died with honor."

"What comfort is honor if he is dead? What good is a good death to a dead man?"

"It is a last comfort," said Isurus.

"But is it?" Taurus rounded on his cousin. "Is it a comfort?"

"To some, it is."

"Not to me. Poison? For him? It is not right."

"There is nothing to be done about it now," said Isurus, with a flicker of steel.

"Yes, there is. I shall go cast the *ra-anara* to Altimus's feet and see him take it up, against his honor."

Isurus threw Hattie a glance of alarm. "Taurus, he'd kill you."

"Is death too great a price for one's honor?"

"Altimus would only have the pleasure of being rid of another threat to his throne, and that your own doing."

"I am quicker than he—and angrier." Taurus was growing unreasonable. Hattie had heard that same wild note in the voice of a twelve-year-old boy in Roke Point who had to be held back from running to the docks after his father's boat was lost.

"Do not deceive yourself," Isurus replied evenly. "You would not have a fool's chance in single combat with him." Hattie's heart ached at the calm in his voice. She knew he felt as Taurus did.

"I have told you, I care for none of that! Galeio will not go unavenged!"

The calm cracked. "And I say that you shall not face him! I forbid it!"

Taurus broke down and stood there, above the bright mosaics, crying.

Isurus looked back at Hattie the way a man would reach out to steady himself against a wall.

When he turned back to Taurus, he spoke quietly. "Where is Mokarran?"

"He shut himself away. But he will see you if you wish it." Taurus took a shaky breath and turned away as he composed himself.

"Go, tell him I wish to see him."

Hattie stared at the gaudy flowers blowing in the breeze and listened to the sound of Taurus's retreating footsteps on the stone path.

The gardens were too warm, even in the shade, and had begun to swim. Hattie cast about for a seat, but at her first step, the world went hot and dark.

She stayed in place and waited for the darkness to pass. The heat had affected her more than usual the last few months.

"Hattie?" Isurus looked to her and his face changed swiftly.

He took her elbow in his hand and led her to a bench. "What is it? Are you ill?"

"I am a little warm, that is all. It—it hasn't been an easy

morning."

"No, you are remarkably pale. Let me get you a drink."

"I don't need any," Hattie protested, holding onto his hand. "It will not help."

"Why? What is wrong?" He knelt down, searching her face as if for signs of danger.

"Nothing is wrong," she said softly. "Only…I was not going to tell you so soon. Not before we had finished and the danger was over."

"Tell me what?" His face was plaintive, bordering on hurt, as if he had done something wrong.

She took his hands between hers and looked up at him, taking a deep breath. "We are three, now."

His face went suddenly grave. "You mean a child?"

"Yes."

His face remained solemn, but he began to rub her hand, gently. "How long have you known?"

"I suspected the night we held memory for Crestus. I am sure now."

"So long...."

"I wanted to tell you." She reached up and brushed his hair off his forehead. "But you carry so much on your shoulders already. I didn't want you to worry before you needed to know. I was going to tell you after."

"I see."

"Don't let it worry you."

He kissed her hand, and the wistful manner that he had carried with him in Roke Point returned.

"I cannot promise that. But I am glad—very glad—to know."

He sat in deep thought a moment, his face darkening.

"I love you, Hattie," he said at last, and his face was light again.

The shimmering red of the dying sun lit the floor and the walls of the open hall of Sphyrna and bathed the white of Hattie's dress in rich gold.

Aeris, as the oldest left among them, carried the token of memory. They could not use a young shark, as those were raised in the runs, but he carried a wreath of white flowers, painted with streaks of blue.

Hattie and Zyaena and Tryaena stood on one side, with their white dresses and armbands, and to their left stood the others: Isurus, Mokarran, Taurus, and Aeris, with the wreath.

Behind them a short distance, Vulpinus stood watching, leaning on his spear.

And Isurus began to sing—softly, lest his voice carry over the water. Hattie had never loved his voice more.

"As the sun goes down to the sea and the seas return to the springs where they were born, so we bid you go, go with the sun, and to joys unknown."

"Farewell, farewell," they answered him. "We shall meet on the dawn."

"As the great sharks come to feed and leave again and return in their season with young, so we say farewell for a time, for in the dawn we shall be with you also." A tear slipped down Isurus's face, but his voice never wavered. Taurus was weeping openly.

"Farewell, farewell," they echoed. "We shall meet on the dawn."

"And so farewell, and so farewell!" Isurus's voice grew softer, rather than louder, but the words he sang were fierce. "To the golden city shall we go and in the dawn meet one another again. And so farewell."

"We shall laugh, we shall feast, we shall forget griefs forever in a river of beauty," they all sang, as if the promise was just within reach, as if their fingertips were brushing it. "And so farewell!"

Aeris stepped forward and set the wreath on the water. "We shall meet on the dawn," he said gently.

The wreath was weighted with stones, and it sank slowly, the paint running in little rivers of blue as it went down through the clear water.

"And so farewell," whispered Isurus.

The thing was done, and one by one, they went down to the water and washed the blue paint from their face and arms.

Aeris lingered beside the water after the others had left, his wistful face illuminated by the ruddy light.

Hattie went nearer to him. He had always been less open than the others, less quick to speak his mind. "Will you be all right?" she asked him.

Aeris sheathed the wistful expression as a tiger might pull in his claws, his face returning to its accustomed stoicism. "I just hope it was worth it," he said.

NINETEEN

Parida

They left just after dawn, in the cool, promising morning, when
the sunlight was streaming down in shafts between the greenery and
stone arches.

Her farewell with Isurus was brief: a kiss, a smile, a see-you-when-
it's-over.

And he had left, dressed in splendid blue and white, with Taurus
and Mokarran, all with gold in their ears and on their necks.

And the waiting started.

The house was quiet. Hattie heard the distant murmur of the
servants at their work, of restive animals, of the noise from the streets
floating in through the vast air above the courtyards, but there was no
sound that held belonging for her.

She climbed to the roof, the only part of the house wholly lit by
the warm, early morning, and looked around her.

She had never been up here in the daytime—only once, briefly,
when it was dark. Now the city lay stretched out around her in the sun,
moving with the regularity of an anthill. The market milled brightly,
and fishing boats already stood in the cut-gem waters around the city.
Nearer at hand stood the halls of the Shark Kind, separated from the
rest of the fine houses and palace grounds by hedges and gates. The
sun sparkled off the shark runs, in contrast to the wild, untamed water
just beyond—the real sea, running toward rocky cliffs. A smooth crease
indicated a current, running like a great river through the center of the
otherwise deep, mottled water.

The current of Athol, the Atlanteans called it. Isurus had told her that it led to a forbidden place, a great cliff under the water, where the sea floor dropped away, hundreds of fathoms down, and the current would drag a man straight to the bottom.

Even Hattie, born and bred beside the murky, fretful Atlantic, shuddered at the mere thought.

A shadow shifted in the green and dark-blue streaked water.

"Mokarran!" It was Zyaena's voice.

She peered off the roof and into the courtyard as Zyaena came through the great doors.

"They have left!" Hattie called down. "I am here alone."

"Hurry! Come down, I must speak with you!"

A knot of dread—the sort she had been trying to hold off all morning—began in her stomach.

"It was a man? You are sure?"

"Yes." Zyaena was wringing her hands, but her face was still forcibly cold and calm. "It was a man's voice. He agreed on a signal."

"But they were all here at the time you heard it. I saw them prepare—" Hattie's heart began to thunder. "All except Aeris."

"And Vulpinus?"

Hattie nodded. "He was here too. Isurus doesn't let him leave the house."

"Then it is Aeris." Zyaena sounded like she had been stabbed.

"Would he betray them? To their deaths?"

Zyaena's face had gone terribly white, her cheeks alone flushed with feeling. "There are worse things than death. Any one of us would strike off our hand for the good of Atlantis. And to keep the Sun

Throne from the hands of one who could destroy it—Hattie, if he has come to believe that Isurus is the Doom—"

"We must warn them."

"How long have they been gone?"

"Less than half an hour."

"I will go and warn them."

Hattie grabbed Zyaena's arm. "Will they not suspect you? It would be more natural for me to follow, as his wife."

Zyaena only blinked. "Isurus would not forgive me if I let you go."

"That will be between him and me." Hattie picked up her light wrap and wound it around her shoulders.

"Then you will not go alone. It will not be safe in the streets."

They never made it. Halfway to the palace grounds, the din of shouts and battle assaulted their ears and Isurus met them alone, blood running down his face and staining his pure white tunic.

"Hattie, what are you doing?" Isurus seized her by the shoulders as if to shield her.

"We came to warn you. It's too late?"

The expression on his face gave her all the answer she needed.

"Where is Mokarran?" Zyaena demanded.

"I thought he was with me." Isurus whirled about looking behind him. "I swear he was at my side."

He turned on his heel to go back.

"Isurus, no!" Zyaena's voice was sharp. "There's no going back."

Already a cluster of soldiers was starting up the street after them.

Isurus fairly pushed Hattie before him. "Run! They will cut us off."

Zyaena threw a despairing glance backward. "Where are the others?"

"They are not coming." It was all he said, and it was clear he would say no more.

Halfway up the road, they met Tryaena with Taurus, who was streaming blood from one arm. They had come from the barracks, where they were to have created a disturbance to draw off the Black Tips.

"They have played the *parida*," he gasped. "They were expecting us."

Tryaena's green eyes churned like a sea in a storm. "Who was the traitor?" she demanded.

Isurus did not answer. "If you come from there, they will have cut off the fisher's street."

"And the merchant's street as well." Tryaena tightened the strap on her knife belt. "The House of Sphyrna is lost to us, and no other will dare take us in. I can get you to Carcharhinus."

"They have us cut off."

"I said I can get you to Carcharhinus." Tryaena's voice took on a sharp edge, and she pushed past them into a narrow, dangerous-looking alley.

She led them through a servant's door, then down a flight of stairs, through a corridor, and up another, and they were again out in another street, the blazing sun beating down on their heads.

Tryaena threw Isurus a swift glance. "Run. I'll cover the rear."

Isurus led the way up the street, running, to a tall house of white stone, its brass-bound doors painted blue as the sea. The crest above the door was a shark, twisting out of the water.

The doorkeeper opened to them at the first thud of Isurus's fist.

The shouts of the pursuing soldiers filled the narrow street, swallowing up all else.

They crowded through the doorway, Tryaena dashing in last of all, and the doors shut on the hot street.

In the sudden silence of the courtyard, the truth hit Hattie like a breaker.

The throne was lost.

"Are you well?" Isurus bent down, peering into her face, for the moment concerned with nothing else.

She nodded and pushed her windblown hair out of her eyes.

Tryaena was shouting orders. Servants barricaded the door.

"Mokarran is out there somewhere." For the first time, Hattie saw Zyaena's stern exterior waver. "The fool—he probably went to find me!"

The girl ran to Tryaena, who snapped her fingers for one of her guards. "Go to the chambers of Prionna and the surrounding gardens. Find the lord of Sphyrna, if you can, and bear him safely back."

The guard departed.

"He is one of my very best." Tryaena's sharp voice gentled for a moment. "If your brother is not dead, he will find him."

"How long can we hold here?" asked Isurus. "Altimus will have reinforcements within the hour."

Tryaena turned to him, her manner quiet but decided. "You are not staying."

"We are surrounded. The tunnels will be guarded."

"You think that we, the guardians of your house and preservers of your life, have no secret ways? There are ancient paths below the sea that the Black Tips have never seen."

"This is my fight." Isurus's voice was low, earnest. "I cannot leave others to suffer an ill fate in my place."

"This is your brother's fault, not yours." Tryaena bound back her thick, bright hair as she spoke. "You have done nothing but your duty. Atlantis will see that usurper banished yet." She whipped her glance around, and her eyes lit on Taurus, trying to bind up his bleeding arm on his own. "There are healers, my lord! Go and see them, before you are left behind!"

Her voice held no sympathy.

"That cousin of yours is hardly fit to be king, and everyone knows it. Fate be hanged. We are the king's people, and fate will not pry our fingers from the true line."

Isurus gave a sympathetic glance in Taurus's direction. "I will wait for him."

"If you do not leave soon, they will cut you off in the hills. I do not even think you should wait for the lord of Sphyrna. We will buy you as much time as we may, my house and I."

"Tryaena, you should come with us. A traitor's death is the best any of us can expect now."

"It's all right." She looked up at him with a small smile. "They will not be taking me alive."

Hattie's heart caught in her chest.

Isurus's jaw tightened. "That is not what I meant."

"I know. But we cannot choose what life gives us. Please—let me do this for you, sovereignty, even as my father did for yours." Her face was sweet, like a girl asking her father for a favor.

Isurus searched her face for a long moment, then pressed his fist to his shoulder. "So be it."

"There are horses." Tryaena indicated with her head to the far end of the courtyard, facing the gardens.

"Hattie." Isurus's sudden use of her name startled her out of her numb listening.

She found her voice haltingly. "Zyaena should not be alone."

In the midst of the preparations for a fight, the swift orders, the clank of spears, the rush of sandaled feet, Zyaena stood like a statue of marble, watching the activity as if it had nothing to do with her.

Isurus hesitated only for a moment. "I will find Taurus."

A servant brought out light armor, and in the middle of the dusty stone floor, Tryaena made ready.

"I suppose you heard the talk, one way or another," said Tryaena, loosing the clasps on her earrings, "that I loved Isurus."

It was the first time she had spoken to Hattie since her arrival in Atlantis.

"Yes."

"Well, it is true, though he never loved me." Tryaena took a leather breastplate and heaved it over her head. The servant cinched it tight from the back. "I think it runs in our blood, this love for the Lamnidaes." The woman gave a grim laugh. "But it is our fate to die for them. That too, seems to run in our blood."

Hattie did not know how to answer this, so she only nodded.

Tryaena took an arm guard and strapped it on tightly. Her eyes met Hattie's, open and honest for the first time.

"Keep him safe. Some men's fault is to run from death…his is to stand between death and his people. Fight for him when he won't fight for himself."

A shout from across the flagstones arrested their attention. Mokarran, dusty and bloody, was casting his arms wide, and Zyaena was running for him.

Something in Hattie's chest gave in relief.

Tryaena's voice drew her attention back. Her tone was flat and hard. "You need to go."

"What you said—" Hattie met her green gaze. "I will. I swear it."

"Hattie!" Isurus reappeared, and Taurus was beside him, his arm bound by a bloody cloth. The servants were bringing out packs of food and fresh clothing, binding them on the horses' backs.

They waited for her.

"The light of the sun be upon you." Tryaena gave her armguard a savage tug.

Hattie forced her voice to be steady. "And on you."

The woman gave a single nod and reached for her spear. That was the last Hattie saw of her.

Victory, even assured, could be made hollow. When word of the traitor's game had come to him from the Master of War—the sea sing his soul to rest—he knew that his brother's end was near. But he had wanted for tonight to be the night he raised his glass of wine in victory, spit upon the memory of the traitors, and went to sleep knowing it would be the last of Atlantis's troubles.

Instead, his brother, slippery as an eel, had eluded him once more.

"It is over," she had said, and it was.

And yet victory, tonight, felt hollow.

There was a lily upon the table. When a hero died, lilies were laid out in memory—this one was for the Master of War, whose last act had been the saving of the Sun Throne.

"Seek beauty." His mother had said that. He picked up the lily gently and studied the petals, white as goat's milk.

"Seek beauty," she had said, "for in beauty we remember the goodness in the world."

It was better that she was gone. She would not have understood that what he had to do was necessary, for the good of Atlantis.

Yet in this moment, he wanted her back more than he ever had.

TWENTY

Fate Is King

Isurus had been standing on the beach, staring at the muted sea under the gray sky, for an hour.

They had traveled all night, among the cliffs and hills, to a quiet cave facing a small inlet. A safe place, Mokarran had said.

It was morning now, pale and forlorn.

Five of them were there, all that was left: Isurus and Hattie, Mokarran, Zyaena, and Taurus. Hattie prepared breakfast, as she was the only one with much practice cooking; even so, it was only flatbreads and the crabs that had been caught in the shallows.

"Isurus…." She went to him, stood behind him. The wind played in his dark hair. "Dearest, you should eat."

He let out a long sigh. "I don't think I can." He turned and gave her an apologetic smile.

Hattie planted her feet. "You need to keep your strength up."

As if to make a compromise, he reached out and took her hand.

The sea shimmered blue-green in defiance of the gray sky. In Maine, such a sky would have darkened the waves.

"It was Vulpinus who saved me. I wouldn't be standing here without him." Isurus's face was very still and quiet.

"What happened?" She wasn't even sure she wanted to know.

"He noticed a signal that Aeris used. It was common among the Black Tips. I would not have known it, but he did. He told me we had to leave, and—and then Aeris tried to detain me. I only escaped with my life because Vulpinus stayed behind, faithful to the last. It was Aeris who betrayed us."

His voice nearly failed him.

"Because of the prophecy?"

Isurus nodded. "It is no longer simply a ruse to keep me from the throne. I think they believe it—that they are the heroes of the prophecy. And the people, too, believe them."

"Do you?" The question came from her mouth unexpectedly, as if put there by something outside of her mind.

Isurus was silent for a long moment. "I cannot deny the possibility that they may be right."

A gust of breeze made her hair stream longingly toward the sea. The wind seemed itself to be crying.

"Hattie, where did I go wrong?"

"You didn't," she whispered earnestly. "You didn't. You chose the right things. And yes, it went wrong, but it doesn't mean that you did wrong."

His eyes were uneasy like the sea when they met hers. "Hattie, I don't want to lose you, watch your hope fade slowly. I don't want to tell you these things."

"It doesn't matter," said Hattie stolidly. "I don't believe them. And I will not, not if that Fate itself comes and tells me."

"Moraire," he said very gently. "Do not speak her name, Hattie. Please."

Taurus had picked flowers, flowers from among the rocks, for the dead.

Mokarran scorned the idea, for Taurus had insisted on including Aeris the traitor, and Vulpinus, whose hands had certainly been stained with innocent blood during his days of service to Altimus.

But Hattie stood with him at the water's edge, in the surf spray, as he sang the words at sunset, quiet and faltering.

Even without paint and without the traditional clothing, it was moving. More so, perhaps, since it was only Taurus, singing alone.

Hattie threw the flowers into the water, doing the duty of the lead mourner among the women. They were beautiful, spindly white flowers, and they sank after a minute or two.

But she could see them still, drifting about in the clear water.

"The food is hot," Zyaena called from the mouth of the cave. "Come and eat."

"In time." Taurus tossed a sorry excuse for a smile over his shoulder. He turned to Hattie, giving her hand a brief squeeze in thanks.

Hattie came back to the fire, her hair and dress windblown from the dark front that was rolling in over the water.

"I do not understand Taurus," she said, as Zyacna laid out the bread, flat and fire-baked. "He takes no thought for tradition until someone has died, and then heaven and earth cannot move him from his purpose."

Zyaena smiled sadly. "Some say that after death, ceremony is of little matter, for once dead, your honor cannot change. Others believe that honor is the greatest gift that can be given to the dead." She brushed her hair out of her face and stirred the fire. "Every man believes something."

"And Aeris believed that fate is king." Hattie said it slowly, reluctantly.

"Aeris believed that to fight on behalf of the Doom would be to fight the inevitable and lose his honor. It is hard to blame a man for that, though the heart rises against his treachery."

"And Vulpinus?"

"He valued what he saw before him over fate. His loyalty was bound to his duty as a soldier. He won his honor in fighting against fate with Isurus."

"So there are many ways to find honor." Hattie leaned her arms on her knees with a sigh. "Do you know what Isurus believes?"

Zyaena did not meet her gaze. "He is your husband, Hattie. Should you not ask him yourself?"

Hattie gazed through the slick, hot air rising from the fire to her husband's solemn frame, facing the sea.

She had thought she knew what he believed. Now, she was less sure.

Word came the following day, through the House of Sphyrna, that the king wanted to meet and talk peace terms. Mokarran had ways of gathering information even in hiding, it seemed.

Hattie was against it from the first.

"I am the loser of the conflict," Isurus explained. "I haven't much of a choice."

"You can stay in hiding," she urged, kneeling down beside him on the beach. "It has the smell of a trap."

"He knows how few of us there are." Isurus traced the pattern of a wave in the sand as he spoke.

"Why then does he want to talk terms, if not to draw us into the open and stamp us out?"

"He wants something beyond stamping us out. If he can be rid of me and keep the throne, it may be that he will forget his anger for the rest of you in time."

"You are not walking into his hands." Hattie stood up, dusting the sand from her skirt.

"No, I will not." Isurus met her eyes with a promise. "But I will meet and speak with him."

"Isurus." He scrambled to his feet as Mokarran came up behind them, his arms folded. Mokarran jerked his chin in summons. "It's a long way to the gate."

"You are coming with me?"

"I would not dream of being elsewhere."

"I am coming too." Hattie drew herself up. She was not letting him out of her sight, not when Altimus was involved.

Isurus gave her a nod of assent. "I'll go put on what little finery I have," he said with a wry smile. "Mokarran?"

"On the contrary, I want to wear as little as possible." Mokarran's voice was dry as he hitched his tattooed shoulders.

They met on the wide spit of sand that Isurus had called the gates when Hattie first arrived in Atlantis—the place where Galeio had brought them on that first lonely night. Isurus's party traveled through the paths below the water, while Altimus's arrived by sea in boats.

Prionna was with the king, her pale eyes gleaming in the sun, and they were escorted by several Black Tips. Behind them, grave and silent, came the Lord of the Shark Kind and his Keepers.

The warm sea-wind whipped about the flat spit, setting their clothes pulsing like flags in the wind. Isurus wore black, with no ornament but an earring. Mokarran stood at his side with arms folded, wearing a kilt with a gold collar and earring, his broad stingray tattoo on full display.

Altimus stopped some ten or twenty feet from them, and the Shark Kind took their place to one side, between the king and the challenger. Hattie held her hair back from her face with one hand.

"Brother," Altimus greeted with a smile. He was decked in the golden regalia of a conquering sea-king. Prionna, spartan-like, wore a plain white dress and jewelry in her hair and ears.

Isurus acknowledged his brother with a mere nod. Mokarran did not try to mask his disgust; Hattie had never seen a sharper or more knife-like expression.

The Lord of the Shark Kind spoke first.

"You have much to answer for, Isurus Lamnidae." The wind whisked at his robes and his thick hair, but his face and his eyes were immovable as stone.

"In what way have I sinned, save that I obey the blood within me and strive to keep the oaths I swore to protect and defend my people while life is in me?"

Prionna accused him next, her voice rich and calm and ruthless. "You have caused fear and confusion and are bringing doom upon the whole of Atlantis by your grasping schemes, even as it is written."

Mokarran was far gone. He spit derisively into the sand.

If the Lord of the Shark Kind noticed, he did not acknowledge it.

"Can you deny that this bloodshed was of your doing?"

"No," admitted Isurus. "But it is clear that my brother knew of my intentions and waited for the last possible moment to reveal his knowledge. Had he confronted me sooner, this would not have happened. And had my plans been successful, there would have been little or no bloodshed."

"But it was of your design," said the Lord of the Shark Kind relentlessly. "Therefore the guilt is yours."

Isurus took the blame silently, but beside her, Hattie heard a clear noise of disapproval from Mokarran.

"I said I would defend Atlantis against any man," said the Lord of the Shark Kind. "I must now fulfill that oath and require a reckoning of you, Isurus Lamnidae."

"Let it be known that the deaths of Tryaena Carcharinus and Vulpinus Alopias are not on my head," said Isurus. "Their choices were their own."

"They fought fate." Altimus's voice rumbled deep in his chest. His massive arms were folded, mirroring Mokarran's. "When you raise your hand against the Last Atlantean, you will be struck down."

Hattie had not intended to speak, but in the face of Altimus's arrogance, anger rose up and burst out of her mouth. "You are not the Last Atlantean. You are a wicked man who hides behind a woman's skirts and uses her knowledge of prophecies to justify what you want."

Prionna smiled. "Can you deny the prophecies? Your man is the Doom. He may fight, but if he wins, he will only destroy the last of his people and bring death upon Atlantis and himself."

"I can and I will deny them," Hattie said stoutly. "I am no Atlantean by blood. I am not afraid, as Atlantis is. Your lies may work on every other person in this kingdom, but they don't work on me."

It was only a slight shift in Prionna's eyes, but Hattie could see the words hit home.

"I will not have idle talk," said the Lord of the Shark Kind. "There must be recompense for the grief brought upon Atlantis, and there must be an end to this struggle before we are destroyed. I therefore demand that there be held a trial—the *sacitha,* to determine kingship."

"Agreed," said Altimus, confident and too quick.

Mokarran opened his mouth too late to protest.

"Agreed," said Isurus quietly.

Hattie felt that her heart ought to be sinking, that she ought to be afraid now. But instead she felt distant, distant as the blue horizon you had to shade your eyes to see.

Nothing could touch her in this moment.

"So shall it be, three days hence. I shall expect both of you to come into custody on the second day for the ceremonial preparations."

"So shall it be," Altimus smiled, the victory light already coming into his eyes.

Isurus's eyes flicked briefly to Hattie's face, and there was resignation in them. "So shall it be."

TWENTY-ONE

"To Lucasta, Going Beyond the Seas"

Of the day that was left to them, Isurus spent much of it with Mokarran. They talked long of the state of the kingdom, and—Hattie assumed, for they walked away to speak of it—what must be done should Isurus lose the *sacitha*.

But come evening, as the golden light of the fading sun closed on their last day together, Isurus took Hattie by the hand and they walked away up the sand, beside the cliffs.

The sea washed against their feet, warm and comforting.

When they had walked awhile in silence, Isurus said, "I have something that I would like you to do, in the event of my death."

Her chest tightened, refusing the thought fiercely, but she only turned a waiting face to him, encouraging him to go on.

"Below the ceremonial runs where the *sacitha* will be held tomorrow, there is a passageway. It leads to a sacred place, beneath the halls of the Shark Kind, which is bound from all but the highest in Atlantis. I need you to go there."

"Yes?" She did not know why her heart was pounding now, after she had been so strangely calm all day.

He reached into his shirt and pulled out a small key on a chain. "This will open the door."

"And what then?"

"Beneath the floor is a vault, marked by a design of gold. You must look there, and you will find a casket. Take what you find inside to the Lord of the Shark Kind and ask him for sanctuary. He will protect you and our child from Altimus."

"What is it?"

"A relic, entrusted to the kings of Atlantis. It is supposed to grant power and might to the bearer. Whether or not that is true—" he gave a humorless laugh— "it will be reason enough for the Lord of the Shark Kind to keep his word."

"I still wish you were not going," she said, softly.

"If there was another way, I would take it."

Her throat was tightening in earnest now, the emotion she hadn't felt before flooding in without warning. "I don't like to think about it happening to anyone. It's barbaric."

"And I am sorry that I have to do it." He reached up and tucked a strand of her hair back that was blowing in her face. "I bring you here to this foreign place, give you a child, and then go and do a dangerous, savage thing—"

"It isn't that I mind. I agreed to this when I said I would marry you, and I don't regret that." She looked down for a moment, watching the foam cast up by the waves and a piece of light green seaweed caught on a rock, waving like it wanted to go back to the water but couldn't. "I just wish I could protect you from this. And I can't."

"You needn't feel responsible for protecting me." His voice was gentle. "I will be all right, you know."

Hattie wished she could believe it.

They walked on in silence, listening to the waves—somewhere in the wind above the cliffs, a white sea bird cried, bathed in the golden light.

"There was a piece of poetry, I think, in your brother's book— 'Though seas and land betwixt us both, our faith—'"

"'Our faith and troth, like separated souls, all time and space controls.'" Hattie smiled, leaning her head against his shoulder. "It's

Lovelace. 'To Lucasta, Going Beyond the Seas.'"

"Yes."

"I did not know you remembered. I returned that book to Fred after a couple weeks."

Isurus chuckled. "You think I cannot commit a thing to memory?"

"Well…."

"My tutor told me more times than I can count that what a boy commits to memory, he knows as a man."

"And what did you commit to memory?" She took his hand, holding it tight, not wanting this evening to end.

"Our histories. The bloodlines of the king's hounds. The story of the First Atlantean. And how to win as the king in *ta-para-rex*. I became so good at that that Mokarran refused to play with me anymore when we were fourteen."

Hattie laughed. She could imagine Mokarran doing that.

He let go of her hand and clasped both of his behind his back thoughtfully. "I wish I did not have to say more, Hattie, but I must."

"Go on." She had no desire to hear it either, but she could not fight him when all the world was against him.

"I am now, in the minds of most, the Doom of Atlantis. I will not ask you to believe it—I understand that is all bosh to you."

Hattie chuckled, hearing the word come out of his mouth. She would take any chance to laugh with him that she could now. Their chances were slipping away like sand in a glass.

"But I am tied to Atlantis by my vows, and those are only broken by death. If I die, Hattie, I want you to raise the child to take my place. Taurus knows what must be done, and he will be only too glad to do it if it keeps him from the throne."

"You aren't going to die, Isurus. You are coming back." She meant to state it firmly, but her voice was strangely unsure. It sounded more like a question than a reassurance.

"Nothing is promised us, Hattie." His voice was low. "I do not want to dash your hopes. And I want Atlantis to be safe, if I am gone."

"Is this what you were talking about with Mokarran? What to do if you don't make it out of the trials?"

"More or less." Isurus gave a wry tilt to his head. "Mokarran is loyal as the air I breathe, and the blood in his veins is quick and hot. Should I die, he wishes to make a brave end with his king."

"Would Altimus kill him?"

"Perhaps. But the House of Sphyrna is powerful. If anyone can weather this storm and survive the aftermath, it will be Mokarran." He laughed low in his throat, more in pain than in humor. "I mean to leave tonight. Altimus will not expect me, so there will be no treachery. But Mokarran—unless I leave in secret, he will surely come with me."

"Just promise me one thing." Hattie's voice was firm. "You will not leave without telling me."

The sunlight was nearly gone—amber-colored, but weak—and as he turned to her, it lit half of his long face like a mask.

"I wouldn't dream of it."

She helped him get ready in the early darkness of the night, when the others were asleep and the stars were bright.

Isurus wore the black outfit he had worn to discuss the *sacitha* and the gold bands that marked him as lord of the House of Lamnidae. He led his horse down to the beach, to the edge of the surf. His face was steeled for his journey, as if he had already left them behind.

He checked the straps on the sheath strapped to his leg, tightened the saddle girth, smoothed his hair once more.

"Dearest, let it be." Hattie reached up automatically to fix it, for he had only managed to muss it more. "It's not going to be any better out there in the wind."

"No," he admitted with a smile.

He thrust his foot in the stirrup and rose into the saddle, firmly checking the impatient horse. It backed and stamped a little in the surf. "Stand," he commanded, quiet and sharp.

He was silhouetted against the night sky, surrounded by stars, the moon lighting his proud face. And for a moment, Hattie saw him as he must have been as king: distant and beautiful, strong as the sun and dangerous as the sea.

"I'll be off now, Hattie." His eyes took in her face as if trying to memorize her in this moment. Then he leaned down from the saddle and kissed her, and she let the moment linger.

"Be careful," she warned.

The smile he gave her was wistful. "Always."

Murmured voices in dark halls. Sheltered lamplight behind curtains. The cold chill of long-dead stone. He saw him across the room, kneeling upon the cool ground, his dark head bent between narrow shoulders as they anointed him with the perfumed water—preparing him for death, the death that was inevitable.

The dark one. The young one. The Doom.

He bowed his own head and crossed his arms as they sprinkled the sweet, scented water over his mighty head and shoulders. For him, this was a pleasantry only, a bowing to tradition as its hero.

Today was not the day he would die.

Today, he would save Atlantis.

TWENTY-TWO

Blood in the Water

The sea cast itself against the sandy shore in a rush of foam and slunk back with a cowed hiss. If Hattie closed her eyes, it almost felt like Maine again.

At dawn, when Mokarran had awoken to find Isurus gone, he had taken a horse and ridden off after him. No pleas to wait or listen to good sense had prevailed. Zyaena had let him go, but Hattie had seen the look of sad finality in her eyes as he rode off.

She brushed her fingers through the sand and leaned her head against her knees. How many times had she done this in her life? Sat beside the ocean, let her troubles settle with the slow rhythm of the waves going in and out?

The sea had always given and taken in her life. Because of the sea, she'd grown up with food on the table, her father and brothers had work. It had brought her Isurus and taken away Jack. Not a year had gone by that it hadn't claimed its toll. But it had always been there, and when she was lonely or afraid, she went to the sea.

"You've been out here a long time." Taurus came up behind her, folded his arms, and looked down at her with a little smile.

"I come to the sea to think."

"No wonder you married Isurus. That was always his way."

"But not yours?" She smiled back, weary as she was.

Taurus shrugged and looked out at the sea. The sun was bright and brilliant, stretching its still, hot rays over the cool blue. He lowered himself down beside her and began tracing spirals in the sand.

Hattie shook her head. "How can you manage to smile when

everything is so bad?"

He laughed faintly. "We are taught from childhood to smile in the face of danger. It is a weakness of mine that I smile at all times."

"I don't think it's a weakness."

He shook his head with amusing solemnity. "It must be because you are foreign."

Foreign. She remembered Galeio's words, the night before his death, about Isurus washing up on a foreign shore just so he could find and marry her. The words had been sweet then; now the memory of them ached inside her.

Her next words came out haltingly "Taurus, how much do you believe in fate?"

He ceased his spirals, resting one arm over an up-drawn knee, and scratched the back of his head. "There is no simple answer to a question like that."

"Go on." Her voice sounded miserable, even to herself. "I have all the time in the world."

"I think that many things happen to us without our choosing," he began slowly. "No man has the power to control everything."

"Do you believe that Isurus is the Doom?"

He scratched his head again, thoughtful. "I've never seen the use in thinking that way. That's where all the heroes in the legends go wrong, after all. Once you make up your mind about a thing, it begins to shape everything else. He could be."

"Does he think that he is?"

"I put my hand in the shark's mouth to say this, but—"

"Go on, I want to hear it."

"You had the advantage of meeting him in your land. My guess is that he was not altogether himself—or he was free to show a different side of himself than he must here. But he is bound to Atlantis by his upbringing and his oaths. He loves it too much to weigh his own life in the balance against it. He would rather die on the chance that he is the Doom than live with the risk that he will someday destroy us."

"But what if the prophecy is mistaken? Or false?"

"Can you tell the people that?" Taurus looked at her with sadness in his eyes. "With all these portents and coming storms? We cannot change our ways or bend our ancient laws, not for any love or ambition. For Isurus, it is not worth it."

"Isn't that what Altimus has done? Bent the ancient laws?"

"Only if he is not the Last Atlantean."

"That doesn't make sense, and it isn't right." She picked up a pebble and chucked it into the water. It wasn't fair that all this should go against Isurus, when he had only ever wanted to do his people good.

"With the throes of the earth and the unease of the Shark Kind, people are afraid. And they're willing to bear up under Altimus's outrages as long as there's the smallest chance that he is the one the prophecies speak of, who will save them from the reign of the Doom."

"But if Isurus wins today? It will assure his kingship, won't it?"

Taurus shrugged, frowning out at the surf.

"Taurus?" The knot of worry tightened in her stomach.

"It's little more than a show, you know. They are not going to let him win."

"What?" Everything had ceased its movement.

"He didn't tell you that?" Taurus looked as if he had been hit in the face by a wave.

Hattie shook her head.

He put his head in his hands.

Isurus had known he was going to die. He had tried to make the parting easier, not to crush their last moments or steal her courage.

The sea resumed its noise, but louder. It roared in her ears. This child would be like the twins—never knowing the father who loved them with all his heart.

"We have to stop him."

"Stop him?" Taurus's face turned a strange shade of white.

"I don't mean to give him up without a fight."

Taurus threw out a pleading arm. "But what will you do? Altimus will hear nothing you say. Will you tell the Lord of the Shark Kind to his face—" He broke off as if the thing was too terrible to mention.

"No, listen. Isurus told me to go to a room below the Shark Kind's halls and open it. He gave me a key. He said that within was a casket, and that if I took it to the Lord of the Shark Kind, he would be bound by the sacred laws to protect me." With every word, she felt surer of what she had to do. "I will take it to him now and beg him for Isurus's life."

"By the brotherhood." Taurus was aghast, his white face working. "He knew. He knew the whole time and said nothing."

"What do you mean?"

"The Heart of Atlantis. He knew where it was kept, but he never touched it." He shook his head, distressed beyond Hattie's understanding. "I could not have done it."

"Could it save him?"

"I do not know. They say that a king who holds it holds sway over the Shark Kind—yet in the hands of the Doom, it could destroy us. That is why he would not lay hands on it, I'll be bound, though he could have assured his victory with it long ago."

"Will you take me to find it?"

His refusal was emphatic. "Never. It is too dangerous. That room is forbidden, and Isurus told me to keep you safe."

"Taurus, please!"

"No—I will not allow it."

"He told me to do it. I need to be the one who does it."

His eyes went oddly keen, fixing on her with a new clarity. "Because of the child?"

"Who told you that?" She started up from the sand, shaking her skirt off.

"Isurus."

"Isurus! He told you and gave me no indication of it?"

"It was only right. Otherwise, I would expect to be king." A rather faint smile crept onto his face. "And you know how terrified I would be."

"Taurus, I tell you now, if you do not help me, I am going alone."

"Hattie, think of the child! You are both safe right now. You do not know the way, and they will probably be guarding the gates."

"I am going, whether you come or not. I will not abandon Isurus."

"In that case, Isurus can hardly reproach me…." His resolve was faltering.

"No. This once, he will thank you."

Taurus hesitated, then brushed the sand off of his hands. "Get what you need. I will tell Zyaena we are going."

The sea-roads that ran below the sea and led to the halls of the Shark Kind were narrower and older than any Hattie had seen. She could tell that Taurus was afraid—afraid for them both, afraid that they were simply riding into death. But she had always been able to sense danger, and there was something far more urgent inside her now.

Isurus was running out of time.

At last they ran to a dead end, a set of doors.

"Is this it?" asked Hattie.

"This is the entrance to their halls." Taurus dismounted and tied his horse to a ring on the wall. He gave her a look of warning. "Entering this place is forbidden on pain of death, except for those bound for kingship."

"Yes." She looked at him, then set a hand briefly on her middle. "We're perfect."

Taurus still suppressed a shudder. Hattie took the key from around her neck and tried it on the door.

It opened.

He gave her a look, half relieved and half sick, and followed her in.

The halls were dark and damp, and after the pale, swimming light of the sea-roads, it took Hattie a minute to be able to see anything in the murk. "Do you know which direction it is?" asked Hattie.

"Our left…I think." Taurus drew his knife and led the way.

At first, the only noise was the sound of their footsteps, carefully treading the stone of the passageway, but the further they went, the more strongly a second sound joined it. Voices—distant but echoing. Behind them, she thought.

Taurus paused and looked back at Hattie.

"Is there anywhere to hide?" she whispered.

He shrugged. She could see the sweat trickling down his neck.

"We need to hurry." His voice sounded pinched.

They quickened their pace down the hall, the voices still following. At last, Hattie saw it: a great door that looked like it was made from a single blue jewel, bound with greened-over bronze.

The voices were growing louder.

"Altimus," whispered Taurus, aghast. "Quick—" There was a small room beside the door, off to one side; as Taurus pushed her in, her nostrils were overwhelmed with the heavy scent of oil and incense.

Hattie's face was pressed against Taurus's shoulder, and she could smell the salt of his sweat in the fine linen of his tunic. The space was nearly too small for them both—a storage room, she guessed.

Everything was in sharp focus. She felt the smooth floor, the corner of a hard table or surface pressing into her back, one of Taurus's hands holding her elbow. She could smell the wound-bandages on his arm. He was almost entirely shielding her from view.

The voices drew near and stopped just outside the room. A brief flicker indicated that someone had a light. It was the quiet, heavy voice of the Lord of the Shark Kind that she heard first.

"It will open to those who have a legitimate claim to the crown of the Shark King and the Sun throne. You have nothing to fear if your suit is true."

"Is there anything else that may bar me?" This was Altimus's rich voice.

"By your adoption as son of the former king of Atlantis, you will be permitted to enter. But the relics, the presence of the Fate, that is dependent upon your suit, and upon your companion."

"My companion?"

"Is she the true and confirmed living Keeper of the Casket?"

"She is, confirmed upon the death of Galeio Triakidae, former lord of that position." The group shifted—Hattie could not see how many there were, but she glimpsed Prionna's face for a brief moment, pale and proud.

"Then you have no need to fear. The relics will not be denied you."

There was a click and a shifting sound, and by the change of light, she guessed they had gone in.

"It's too late," whispered Hattie.

"Steady," whispered Taurus.

Weariness stole over Hattie as they waited, pain growing in her feet and back. Whatever they were doing was taking a long time, and they were being quiet about it.

"There must surely be a mistake." Altimus's voice came clear to them from within. "I am the sworn king of Atlantis."

"These locks and fates have no regard for outward appearances," came the Lord of the Shark Kind's voice. "There must be a lie somewhere."

"But I am vowed! You accepted my vows!"

"Is Galeio Triakidae dead?"

"Yes, yes! He took poison, he died, he——"

"Did you see his body?"

"No." Altimus's voice was like a stone dropped in a pool of water. "Prionna told me of it. Prionna? Tell him."

"He does not need to be told," said Prionna. "He knows the truth."

"Then why is it not working?" Altimus roared.

"Galeio Triakidae lives," said the Lord of the Shark Kind. "He dwells with us."

Hattie smothered a gasp even as she felt Taurus freeze.

"Traitors." The tone of Altimus's voice was a whisper, but Hattie heard it like he had said it to her face.

"The Shark Kind answer only to Atlantis herself." The Lord of the Shark Kind's voice had not changed one shade. "We owe kings no allegiance."

"But the Fate, the Doom of Atlantis—"

"Galeio Triakidae was not the Doom. What you passed upon him he was not deserving of. Therefore he found a place in the halls of the Shark Kind until such time as is right for him to return."

"You have set yourself against me and aligned yourself with that outcast!"

"The Shark Kind take no sides. If Isurus Lamnidae is the Doom, he will die."

Altimus gave a cry of rage. "Wicked woman! Viper in my wine! How could you do this to me?"

"You brought it upon yourself!" Prionna hissed back, much calmer than he, as if she had been waiting for his rage to be released. "I made you everything you are. You never would have accepted your destiny without my foresight, and yet the one request I made of you, you denied."

"You defied my command, the command of your king—"

For the first time, Prionna's laugh was pleasant to Hattie's ears. "I am your greatest ally, Altimus. I gave you my allegiance before you even knew to demand it as your right. I owe you nothing."

"Where is he?" demanded Altimus. "Bring him down now."

"We may send for him," said the Lord of the Shark Kind, "but the time for the *sacitha* has come. We will attend to this when it is concluded."

Altimus gave a growl. "Very well. There will be time when my brother is dead. And only when he is dead will I forgive this trespass, Prionna."

"How quickly you forget that this is upon your own head," she returned coldly. "I told you that you had stepped beyond the mark we agreed upon, and you would not listen. Here you reap the reward."

"After the *sacitha*," warned Altimus. They passed up the passageway, and their voices faded from hearing.

"Quick, now," said Taurus, stepping out into the hall and hastening to the door.

Hattie raised the key to the hole, and the door opened. She stopped short in the doorway. The room was unlike anything she had ever seen or dreamed of seeing.

The floor was paved with designs of waves and sharks, but all in metal and jewels. The room was circular, two-thirds of it stone, the other third glass that looked out beneath the sea. The sea was pale and brilliant blue near the window, but it grew darker the further out it went, as if it dropped away into a deep abyss.

"It is in the floor, Isurus said so…in the gold."

There it was: an intricate spiral of gold in the very center of the room.

Taurus knelt down and began running his hand over it. "Surely there must be some indication…."

"He didn't say anything else, just that it was underneath." Hattie bent down and looked intently over the spiral. "Is there anything in your stories that would give us an idea what to do?"

"Galeio!" Taurus cried in a sudden, rapturous tone. "Galeio would know! He is the other."

"Can you get him?"

"I shouldn't leave you."

"Nonsense. Shut the door, I'll be all right in here."

Taurus unsheathed his knife and handed it to her. "Just in case." Then he was gone.

It was terribly silent in the room. Hattie stood puzzling over the gold in the floor, hoping to find the catch, but after tracing the spirals a few times, she gave up and went to the window.

The abyss that swallowed up the brighter blue before her was deep and thick; she could only be looking at the current of Athol. That meant the runs where the *sacitha* was—where Isurus was—were almost directly above her.

The nearer sand was pale and soft under the greenish guise of the sea, small schools of fish flitting about, strands of seaweed bending in the currents. Hattie leaned her hand against the glass and looked up at the sun's rays filtering into the water.

It started as a shadow. She thought it was just a place where the sun was blocked from above, but then it stirred, growing larger as it neared the window. Hattie stood rooted where she was, afraid even to move her hand from the glass, watching in mute horror as the shadow materialized into the form of a great shark.

It was almost twice the height of a man and easily broader than a boat, its eyes small in its great face, its gray-blue skin marred and marked with dozens of ancient scars.

She did not need anyone to tell her—this was Moraire, the one they called the Fate.

The shark moved slowly, deliberately toward the glass until it blocked the sea from Hattie's view entirely. Hattie stood unmoving, breathless, looking it back in the face.

And suddenly, within her, the baby began to move. Just a flutter, but Hattie knew beyond a doubt that it was not her.

The world swam a moment and then became very clear—she saw the movement of the water around its gills, its black eyes staring at her, felt the cool of the glass against her fingers. And the shark waited as the child moved again, as if it were a meeting between the two of them and she was simply caught in the middle.

Then there came a rumble as if from a great distance. Slowly, the shark moved on and the child grew quiet.

From above her, as if in a dream, she heard the cry of many voices. The earth trembled.

The *sacitha.*

The sky above the sea was darkening. She watched the darkness filter into the greenish sea and Moraire disappear into the growing darkness.

Hattie turned and ran.

Not a single conscious thought guided her—where she was going, how to get out, what she would do when she got out. It was as if she knew all these things already.

She was panting, feeling faint when she gained daylight—or what should have been. A great bank of clouds blocked out the sun; she saw flashes of relentless lightning, almost constant, but there was no thunder. People were screaming, shouting, and suddenly the ground convulsed, knocking her over.

She dragged herself up, caught the nearest man by the arm as he ran by. "What is it? What has happened? Where is the *sacitha?*"

His face was ashen; he was babbling incoherently.

"Where is Isurus Lamnidae?" she finally shouted, shaking him.

"It's too late," he managed, tearing out of her grasp as another quake rippled the ground. "Isurus Lamnidae is dead."

251

TWENTY-THREE

The Last Atlantean

The ceremonial runs glittered with scattered sunlight, the same sunlight that beat down upon his naked back like an old companion.

Isurus adjusted the hammered gold armbands on his wrists and waited in silence.

The Lord of the Shark Kind and Altimus still had not made their appearance.

There was a crowd: many lords and merchants, some commoners. The silence that hung over the runs was what he noticed the most—you would not think that so many people could be so still.

"Sovereignty." The deep voice sounded from over his shoulder, and he turned to see Mokarran standing before him, clad in kilt and golden net, a blue drop hanging in one ear. His black hair was slick in the blinding sun.

His heart nearly gave. "Mokarran, what are you doing here?"

"I could not let you face this alone."

"You should not have come."

"Do not speak. We understand each other. Let no ceremony stand between us this day."

The words came out thicker than he meant. "I am glad of your coming, Mokarran."

"I brought you this as well." Mokarran held out his knife, long-bladed and handled. It was a prized possession, handed down from father to son, and Isurus knew that Mokarran kept it sharp as a razor.

He held out his hand and Mokarran put the handle in his palm. With a flick of his wrist, Isurus spun the knife, twisted it round, and made a clean stab in the air.

"I know no smith alive who can equal this craft. It will do well."

He pulled his old knife out, letting it clatter to the stones, and shoved Mokarran's into his belt.

A low murmur moved through the crowd and Mokarran glanced over, behind Isurus's back. "They are coming."

"We should say farewell, then. If you see Hattie again—" It wouldn't matter, really. He had already said everything he could say to her. "Well, I suppose she knows."

"Salute Galeio and Crestus for me," said Mokarran, clasping his friend's arm. "Tell them I shall greet them face to face ere long. Tell them I shall make a brave end."

"I shall look for you there."

They parted, and Mokarran disappeared back into the crowd.

A glance back at the water showed the sleek gray shapes of the king's hounds drifting lazily beneath the water. He knew each one of them by name.

Altimus stepped up across the paving stones from him, dressed alike, in a white kilt, with golden armbands. His thick hair was tied back, his muscles gleaming with oil, his eyes glinting with promise of victory.

They had been brothers, once. He did not know this monster, this man who was stealing his inheritance and the hearts of his people.

How cruel was fate to choose a man like this for its hero?

The Lord of the Shark Kind stepped out between them, drawing them both forward.

The cool thumb pressed into Isurus's wrist, and he could sense a great strength that lay dormant in the man.

"Isurus Lamnidae, once king of Atlantis, does challenge the right of crowned Shark King, Altimus Carcharodon, to the throne by daring the *sacitha,* the Test of Kings. Do you consent to this test, my king?"

"I do!" Altimus's voice rang out strong.

"And do you consent to this test, Isurus Lamnidae?"

"I do." His words were stolen away by the wind.

"Then may the pack decide the just claim." The Lord of the Shark Kind raised their arms high, then dropped them. "You shall both swim five lengths, from the near banner to the banner across the run. The man who is left, he is king. So be it."

"So be it." They echoed as one.

The Lord of the Shark King drew his knife and made a small, clean cut on the side of Isurus's heel. It stung like a wasp—an annoyance, but not enough to pull his attention from the water before him.

At least, if he had to die, it would be in the water.

The Lord of the Shark Kind was speaking, but his words were dull; Isurus heard each word like a man who does not understand the language.

Hattie came to his mind, her brown eyes troubled. He had failed her. He had brought her to his home to make her a widow. But he would make this end, if end it must be, brave enough that even history would have to admit that the Doom was a valiant man.

The order came. He tightened his belt hard across his hips, checked his knife, and dove cleanly into the runs.

Clear, warm water rose to meet him, and he struck out for the other side, feeling the familiar resistance of the blue beneath him.

Altimus was two lengths away from him, nearly equal. Altimus was the more powerful swimmer, but Isurus had always been faster. They gained the far side and Isurus whipped around, swift as a shark, and struck out the way they had come. The sharks had begun to circle, merely curious for the moment. After all, they knew these men well.

With every stroke, the bluish water parted, sending spray up like diamonds. Strange, how the clearest thing in his mind right now was the water.

A wave crashed into his side with stunning force and the crowd shouted. He whirled around looking for attack and was met by another wave.

It was not a shark—it was an earthquake.

"Look what you bring upon us!" shouted Altimus, and Isurus had only a moment to dodge before his brother's blade sliced the water beside him.

A shark came up from below, knifing between them, half-mad with the blood smell, bewildered by the shaking of the run.

Another wave hit them both. For a moment the world was twisting bubbles and swirling water, and then he was up, gasping for air, feeling like he had been kicked in the chest.

Altimus was streaming water; he flipped his hair out of his face.

Another tremor moved the earth. Isurus saw the paving stones buckle and ripple. This was no time for a challenge; the run was about to crumble. He struck out rapidly for the edge. Through the fog in his head he heard the people screaming—for the *sacitha,* or for their own lives?

Searing pain shot through his leg. He twisted around even as Altimus withdrew the knife and lunged backward. One of the young sharks closed in, tearing at his bleeding leg, and Isurus drew his knife in a blind flash, stabbing again and again, trying not to see which hound it was, winning his way free even as tears stung his eyes.

"Altimus!" he shouted. Rage and pain filled his head—he could hardly see.

A massive arm seized him and pinned him against the side of the run, a great knee pressing into his hip. "I will not have you endangering Atlantis, endangering my throne." Another shudder shook the world, jarring them both.

The run gave, and the far end that abutted the sea crumbled and rushed out in a swift stream, sucked down into the bottomless depth below. Isurus grabbed hold of the stone on the edge of the run, clinging for life itself. The sea swept past them, pulling, wanting to claim them for its own.

Just beyond cruised a monstrous fin. For a moment, the world stopped and his blood ran cold.

Moraire was waiting for them.

If he let go, they would be washed away into the current of Athol, into the jaws of Moraire.

A flash of pain shot across his face. Altimus was braced with one hand on the rock, the other gripping Isurus. His eyes went to his knife.

"If you live," taunted Altimus, "you'll be too maimed to take the throne."

Hattie's face flashed before his eyes: her bright, innocent smile, the way she clasped her hands behind her back as if she had a delightful surprise, the way her hair curled all on its own.

The pain streaked up his leg into his side, and his face burned like fire with every violent lap of the water against it. The sharp tang of blood was in his nostrils—all he could smell was blood and salt. The strength was draining from his arms; blackness loomed at the corners of his eyes. Altimus gripped him tighter, holding against the pull of the sea, but Isurus saw in his glance the bloodlust of the sharks as he let go of the rock for one moment to reach his knife again.

"It's over, Isurus. Your throne is gone forever."

And in that moment, Isurus saw his chance.

He leaned up toward his brother's face, gasping for the air above water to speak the words.

"I did not come back for my throne," he whispered. "I came back for my people."

He let go, and they fell together.

The world was blue and green, as it had always been since the beginning of time. And there he was, standing before her, and she was a girl, just a girl, reading in the sunshine, with dreams and hopes and ambitions greater than any other girl of Atlantis.

The glare of the sun off the sea lit her like a goddess in the tales, and he could hardly look at her.

"Where is my promise?" he asked her.

"You have what you wished. You have become great."

"Where is my promise?" he asked again.

She laughed and it was sweet, and the scent of salt was in the air.

TWENTY-FOUR

Rise, Hope

Hattie clasped her hand over her mouth, smothering a scream, and stumbled toward the crumbling run. Everyone else was fleeing in the other direction. The water was alive, washing up over the stones now, threatening to knock her over with every tremor of the earth.

Nothing could be seen in the churning water.

"Hattie!" A voice broke out, loud, over the crash of the earth, and before she knew who had shouted, Mokarran had his arms around her, pulling her back.

"Hattie, there's nothing to be done. Stay away from the water."

She did not fight him. He led her back to the steps and she realized somewhere between the sea and the steps that the earth had stopped reeling.

The sea was fretful and roaring, but the world seemed quiet after the rumbling and shaking. Mokarran's black hair was covered in stone dust, and blood trickled down his face as he leaned down to look into hers. "Is it well with you?" he asked with concern.

Hattie swallowed and nodded. There was a strong voice inside her telling her she could not fall apart. Her arm shook as she tried to support her weight on the stairs.

"Where is Zyaena?" Mokarran was asking.

"She is safe, she did not come with me—I came with Taurus—" A thought struck her. "Where is Altimus?"

"He is gone as well." Mokarran's face was drawn, his voice choked with dust and grief. "They both fell to Moraire."

Hattie pressed the back of her hand against her mouth. The

words felt like someone had twisted a knife into her middle. "What now?"

"Do not worry about it now. You are safe."

Hattie coughed; there was so much dust in the air.

"You are well?" he asked again. She had not known he could speak so gently.

"Yes," she replied, though her heart was not in the answer.

She rose and looked out over the water from the vantage point of the stairs. It was no good to look, but she had to.

A monstrous fin was circling, round and round, in the same slow, expectant way she had seen sharks circle an overturned fishing boat back in Maine. "She's still out there," Hattie said, her voice thick.

Mokarran rose and peered out where Hattie was pointing.

He stared hard, then began to scale the nearby statue. "There's something out there, in the shallows before the drop—a sandbar, perhaps—something raised by the throes. It was not there before."

"Why does she circle it?"

"Stay here." Mokarran sounded breathless. He jumped down. "If there is any trouble, go to the Shark Kind."

He ran up to the doors of the hall.

"What is it?" Hattie called after him.

"There's a body on the sand. Please, wait here."

Hattie stood watching as a boat was launched—a large one, for Moraire was already the size of a boat.

Then it began to rain in sheeting torrents, and the wind picked up, whisking the skirt of her dress, soaking her in seconds. She moved up under the shelter of the roof of the hall, her arms clasped around herself, watching the boat.

Before the rain had begun, Moraire had been circling. Now she was gone. Hattie watched the water but saw no sign of her.

The boat's hull drove against the spit, and she could see men climbing down, moving about. It was impossible to tell more from that distance.

It was a long time, or so it felt to Hattie, before they pulled up alongside the ruined run and one of the men jumped from the deck to the pavement to secure the boat.

Mokarran came forward first, to meet her.

He was soaked through, the rain streaming in rivers down his chest, dripping a swift, rhythmic tattoo from his blue earring. "It is Isurus," he said solemnly. "But I do not want you to see him just yet."

"Is he dead?"

Mokarran shook his head.

"Is he dying?"

Mokarran shrugged his shoulders, and for the briefest moment, he looked like a lost boy about to cry.

"I have sent for the best healer," he said.

Behind him, she saw the stretcher lift and pass; she saw a pale face and blood, staining his face, staining the stretcher.

Her whole heart rose into her throat. "I want to see him. I don't care what he looks like."

"And you will," said Mokarran gently. "But since he cannot take care of you right now, I must. Let the healer see him first; let him decide if there is anything that can be done."

Hattie realized she was crushing the soaked skirt of her dress in her hands. She smoothed it down and looked up at Mokarran, controlling her features as completely as any Atlantean woman.

"Take me in, then. I will wait."

She had been at his bedside for the last three hours while they worked, holding one of his hands. He had not woken.

The cut on his face had been sewn; it was ugly, and it was going to scar. She had seen a cut like it once before, a spidery gash that looked like cracked glass. One leg was badly mangled, his chest and arms were gashed, and worst of all, the healer thought something could be permanently damaged in his legs or back. His heartbeat was weak and he was cold, but he breathed.

Hattie remembered how she had helped Mansell stitch up the gash in his leg that evening in Roke Point, how he had not moved an inch under the sailor's needle. There was so much she had not known then.

A throat cleared in the doorway. The healer's apprentice started to his feet, and the surgeon looked up briefly, his hands still for a moment.

Hattie turned to see the Lord of the Shark Kind standing in the doorway, his face half lit by the torches that flanked the entrance. He was rain-soaked, his solemn face marred by the rivulets that ran from his dark hair.

He motioned for them to continue their work and stepped in, crossing the room until he stood at Hattie's shoulder, above Isurus. His fingertips went to his left shoulder, and he bowed his head. He murmured something under his breath.

Then he seemed, for the first time, to notice Hattie. "You are wed to him, are you not?"

"Yes."

"You would have been queen."

Hattie nodded. Even if Isurus lived, the laws of Atlantis would not allow a man maimed by a shark to sit upon the Sun Throne.

"Still, it shall be your line. Moraire chose."

Something fluttered deep inside her. "How do you know?"

"Isurus is alive. Therefore she chose."

She let her breath out slowly. "I see." She would not tell him about her encounter, then. Not yet.

"I was mistaken," he said at last, looking at her, and for the first time she felt she was looking at a man, not a distant, ancient being. "Our kind is rarely fooled, but this time, I will say it—I was mistaken about Isurus Lamnidae."

He looked to the healer. "Will he survive?"

The healer glanced up. "I always said it was hard to kill a Lamnidae. If he wakes up, I think the man will pull through."

"Have a care how you speak of him," said the Lord of the Shark Kind. "It may be that he can no longer sit on the Sun Throne, but he is the Last Atlantean."

A sudden, deep silence took the room, and a prickling warmth washed over Hattie. "Why—why him?"

She was so weary, it was hard to keep her voice straight and steady. "Why is he the Last Atlantean?"

"The prophecy, as we have waited for it, has been fulfilled. With sweet to salt, the tale is ended. In giving his life for Atlantis, he has performed the act, even as Nalak did; and in the same way, his life has been spared."

"But the blue fish, and the sharks, and—"

"If he had not fulfilled it, I would not have spoken it." A flicker of warmth kindled in his eyes. "It is not your task to interpret prophecy."

"No." Hattie almost laughed. She was so tired, so relieved.

The Lord of the Shark Kind set his hand on her arm. "Send word when he awakes. If you are in need of anything that we may provide, the Kind will not withhold it from you."

He touched his forehead and then Isurus's, saying something softly under his breath. Then, silent as a shadow, he passed out of the room.

When Hattie looked in the doorway where he had been, she saw Galeio Triakidae leaning against the doorframe.

"Galeio!" She got up, leaving Isurus's hand for the moment and crossing the room to greet him. Tears sprang to her eyes unbidden.

He smiled and looked down at the ground. "How is he?"

"The healer thinks he may live." Hattie blinked the tears back. "In what condition, they can't say."

Galeio folded his arms and nodded. "He was ever a brave man," he said. "He'll need courage yet."

"What a great deal of trouble one prophecy manages to make," Hattie murmured.

Galeio cleared his throat. His brow furrowed. "I have a request to make. An unpleasant one, I fear."

"Go on." She had faced so much unpleasantness today that whatever it was could hardly rattle her.

"I wish to ask that you spare Prionna, for the service she did for me. It was done selfishly, perhaps, but she preserved my life. And I loved her father."

"And what of the others?"

"The Black Tips you may do with as you wish. Stellarus has fled."

"I don't wish Prionna harmed." Hattie's eyes wandered back to the still form of her husband on the bed. "She has lost a great deal today."

She turned back to Galeio. "May we expect trouble from the Black Tips?"

He shook his head. "I think not."

"Is there anything else I must know?"

"The people will need to be addressed. They must know what has happened."

"I'll talk to them," said Hattie. "I suppose it is my duty. When shall I do it?"

"In the morning. Tell them the truth, but briefly."

"Very well."

"I will be there. Do not worry." He bent and kissed her hand. He threw one lingering look back at Isurus, lying motionless in the bed, but did not go to him.

Hattie walked out into the pale morning sun, half a day and a whole night later, to find Taurus standing at the edge of the water, his arms folded.

"Look," he said, nodding out toward the water with his head.

"What?" She saw nothing but clear blue water. Its troubled tossing had settled.

"The island is gone, washed away by the waves."

"Gone already?"

"It served its purpose." Taurus smiled.

"Taurus, I want to thank you," began Hattie.

"What for? Not all that yesterday?"

"It could not have happened without you."

"I was glad to do it," he said. "I would do it again, not knowing the end."

Hattie smiled. "You would have made a good king, Taurus."

"I would not," he countered. "I am far too wild. Everyone knows it."

She laughed quietly. "When are you going to admit that you're really not as bad as you want people to think you are?"

He ducked his head with a wry smile.

A young voice sounded behind them. "My lady."

It was the healer's apprentice, his head lowered respectfully, blinking a little in the sunshine. "He is awake. He asks for you."

It took a moment for her eyes to adjust again to the dim light. The healer was bent over Isurus, talking intently.

"How is he?" Hattie broke in quietly.

"Hattie?" His voice was thin, like the grease paper in the windows of Starbuck's mercantile.

"I am here," she said, laying her hand over his and leaning over him so he could see her whole face.

His face was white, as it had been when she first met him, his eyes the same shifting-sea color, but warm and belonging, not wary.

"What has happened?"

"You won," she said gently.

Primrose for renouncement, rosemary for remembrance, sea-lavenders for regrets.

A single lily for a hero.

She stood at the edge of the water, the stones hot on her bare feet, looking down at the eternal chasm of the ruins.

The blue, blinding water ran on and on. Like life, from the beginning of time.

"From pride we come, to pride we go...." Her voice was thin against the rushing of the water. "Hear our cry, let us depart in peace."

The water below her roared like a storm.

"Let honor and memory grace us. Forever and ever, for time without end." She pulled the single lily out and dropped it with stony fingers to the burning ground. "Forever and ever, for time without end." She cast the flowers to the coursing sea.

For a single moment, they rose against the hot sky like victory flowers.

The child—Jack, she called him, when it was just family—was quiet and calm as Hattie handed him into the Lord of the Shark Kind's arms, as he painted the customary blue streaks on his face and touched water to the child's lips, sweet and salt.

"May this child be strong. May he bring honor to his country and peace to his house. May the sea ever call him as it calls to each of us, until we go beyond the horizon. May his laughter be loud, his eye bright, and his house plentiful. May he honor our heritage and the shark-kind, and be wise all his days."

"So be it," replied the crowd.

"I give now to the child, king of Atlantis, the name Verus Lamnidae. May his rule be long and prosperous, and may he have the courage of his fathers before him. Long live the Shark King."

"Long live the Shark King!"

Isurus Lamnidae never walked again. The price he paid for his people was his strength and his pride. But there would be no king remembered by his people with greater honor than he; and his sons followed in the ways of their father, good and strong and brave.

As for their mother, there was no one more beloved in all of Atlantis. Her courage without savagery was praised by the wise. And so it was said among the people that Isurus Lamnidae was the Last Atlantean, but it was Hattie Scrow who had made him so.

With Thanks

This was my almost-impossible book. Most of it was drafted and edited while sick, burned out, or grieving. These are the people who made it possible.

James Egan, my cover designer. You continue to blow me out of the water with every book.

My betas and proofreaders, Meg, John, Esther, Lucy, Audrey, Lydia, and Anna. Thank you, thank you, thank you. This was hardly a typical run, but you guys brought it home.

Katie Phillips, who read over this book in its early stages, and whose perspective helped shape it into what it is today.

My incredible street team—you guys truly pack a punch. You're amazing.

My aces in the hole, Lydia and Esther. The passion and excellence in your art and graphics make me look way cooler than I actually am.

My coffee boy, Ethan. You are the man. I still don't know anyone who can pull off coffee and hot chocolate like you.

Special thanks to Schuyler McConkey, Claire Banschbach, Elizabeth Alessio, Cindy Worrell, Mollie Reeder, and Joe Rigney.

To my wing-man Elisabeth, whose time, dedication, and clear sight helped make this book what it is. I wouldn't have nothing if I didn't have you.

To Katherine Alice Ogilvie (1919 – 2020), whose moxie inspired Hattie's. Thanks for the stories.

And to my Heavenly Father, to whom I owe everything. The beauty in every story is because of you.

EMILY HAYSE is a lover of log cabins, strong coffee, and the smell of old books. Her writing is fueled by good characters and a lifelong passion for storytelling. When she is not busy turning words into worlds, she can often be found baking, singing, or caring for one of the many dogs and horses in her life. She lives with her family in Michigan.

Connect with Emily!

Website: emilyhayse.com

Instagram: @songsofheroes

Twitter: @theherosinger

Facebook: /theherosinger

Goodreads: /theherosinger